THE BOOKSHOP AT THE BACK OF BEYOND

THE BOOKSHOP AT THE BACK OF BEYOND

Amy Sparkes

WALKER
BOOKS

First published 2023 by Walker Books Ltd
87 Vauxhall Walk, London SE11 5HJ

2 4 6 8 10 9 7 5 3 1

Text © 2023 Amy Sparkes
Cover and interior illustrations © 2023 Ben Mantle

This book has been typeset in Berkeley Oldstyle

Printed and bound in Great Britain by CPI Group (UK) Ltd

British Library Cataloguing in Publication Data: a catalogue record for this book is available from the British Library

ISBN 978-1-5295-0566-5

www.walker.co.uk

The author will donate 5% of her royalties
for this book to ICP Support
www.icpsupport.org
Registered charity number: 1146449

 For Merrianna

Everyone has secrets, do they not?

Sometimes deep, sometimes dark,

sometimes well-meaning or long forgotten – buried in hidden places.

But secrets will sleep and bide their time.

Because one day, sooner or later, they will wake – and there will be consequences.

The secrets will come out to play.

And those who patiently wait in the shadows, who watch from the windows,

they gather the secrets.

And soon … the game begins.

CHAPTER 1

There was surely a point when life couldn't get much stranger, but Nine wasn't completely convinced she'd reached it yet.

She narrowed her eyes and slowly, carefully, crouched down in the plum-carpeted hallway of the House at the Edge of Magic, facing the front door. The satchel she wore across her body brushed the carpet, her precious music box tinkling inside.

Focus. Just like a cat, Nine was sighting her prey, stalking it quietly, ready to pounce at the right moment. She clenched her fists, stretched her fingers – her pre-pounce ritual.

Nine glared at the little creature, which almost within reach. It was the size of a small rat, with large, round eyes and a body that looked like a blue ball of wool. It sat back on its little hind legs, using its front legs to hold – and nibble – a prize of its own. A prize it had stolen from Nine's plate. But not for long.

Nine was on in three...

Oh, she was going to get her flippin' toast back.

Two...

If it was the last thing she did.

One...

Nine leapt forwards with the determined spring of an experienced pickpocket, her satchel flapping against her hip. But her target seemed equally determined and experienced. The creature gave an indignant squawk, hastily stuffed the toast in its mouth and scrambled away from Nine's outstretched fingertips – as she landed face down on the carpet.

Nine turned her head right to see the blue ball of wool on legs scurrying and leaping up the main staircase.

"Oh no you don't!" she cried, jumping to her feet and making a dash for the stairs.

"Er … Madam," came the voice of a young wizard from the other end of the hallway, "is everything under control?"

10

"Yes, Flabberghast!" snapped Nine, as she half fell up the stairs, the little blue creature escaping her fingertips again. "Perfectly under control!"

"Ah, good, marvellous," said Flabberghast, his tone a little nervous. He wore indigo pyjamas, a pointy indigo hat and fluffy purple slippers and leaned against the kitchen doorframe.

Nine leapt again at the creature, this time half falling *down* the stairs with a not-entirely-perfectly-under-control thump.

The wizard twisted his mouth doubtfully. "I could simply request that Eric makes some more?"

Nine scowled as the blue ball of wool scurried further up the stairs and onto the main landing. She turned her scowl to Flabberghast and pointed her finger at him. "Nobody," she said, "steals my toast." She leapt to her feet once more and hurtled up the plum-carpeted stairs.

The many portraits of Flabberghast's witch and wizard ancestors – all with the same flared nostrils and silvery-sparkling eyes – passed like a blur as Nine chased the creature to the main landing. When she arrived there, she scanned the area furiously.

Dozens of doors of every size and shape dotted the walls. Some were reachable by criss-crossing staircases and landings, some by wooden ladders, and others appeared not to be reachable at all. The different floors were linked by a huge central spiral staircase with a rope handrail that snaked its way up to a distant ornately painted ceiling.

"Where *are* you?" whispered Nine through gritted teeth.

She saw movement out of the corner of her eye. Nine looked up to see the toilet giggling and hopping cheekily across a rickety landing. It had a frustrating habit of wandering about and disappearing, and — sure enough — Nine watched as a door opened and the toilet quickly hopped inside. She tutted and made a mental note of which door it was hiding behind in case she needed it later.

Then came the sound of tiny, toast-stealing, scurrying feet. Nine's gaze shot to the right: a wobbly flight of stairs, which led to a silver door decorated with a curious golden question mark. Her mother's old bedroom.

A cold piece of nibbled toast lay outside it, and a small blue ball of wool was now flattening itself almost entirely before sliding under the doorframe and disappearing into the room.

"No! You are *not* going in there!"

Nine ran to the stairs, her satchel thumping against her. She pounded up the steps so fast that they threatened to collapse. She thrust her hand out towards the iron ring handle that formed the dot of the question mark and twisted it sharply to the right.

As she burst through the door, Nine noticed the faintly familiar scent and took a quick, deep breath – but there was no time to dwell on it. She glanced around the room, searching for the creature. Every wall had a narrow bookcase filled with books, and was painted a bold turquoise. Empty picture frames hung on the walls and an unticking golden clock sat silently on a shelf.

A silver flash at the window beside the bed caught Nine's attention. Outside, the blackness of the World Between Worlds was split by more flashes of silver strands, which rose, twisted together, and then exploded into fading stars. A little fanlight at the top of the window always stayed open – the window Nine had squeezed through once to get into the locked House. A window she had reached by climbing up the footholds and handholds that jutted out of the House's brickwork. As if her ma had done that before her...

"You are absolutely *not* staying in here!" Nine announced to the room.

There was a tiny scrabble of defiance from under the bed. Nine cast her satchel off, causing a tinkle of protest from her precious music box. She dropped flat on her stomach and peered underneath the bed. There were some clothes, a little hooped fishing net on the end of a long wooden handle, and right near the wall, a teapot ... behind which poked out a little blue woolly bottom.

Got you.

Nine slowly moved her arm towards the fishing net until her fingers grasped the handle. One swoop and she would surely catch the creature... Her grip on the net tightened. She fixed her gaze. Her arm muscles tightened in readiness and—

"TEA CUPBOARD!" came Flabberghast's distant voice.

No! Not the tea—

ZAP!

Nine was turned into a rocking horse with a dragon's head and a pig's tail. The blue ball of wool's bottom turned into a bubble that grew bigger – and bigger.

The spell on the tea cupboard was a thoughtful hangover from the curse placed on the House at the Edge of Magic by Flabberghast's sister – the very same one who had imprisoned Flabberghast and the others inside and shrunk it to no more than an ornament when Nine had pickpocketed her bag and found it. The one who had tried on *several* occasions to kill them and who Flabberghast had made quite clear he wanted nothing more to do with. But now the curse had been broken, the witch seemed to have left them in peace, except for the brief reminders every time they touched the cupboard to get some strawberry tea.

The annoying spell began wearing off, as it always did. Nine became more Nine, and the bubble-bottom of the blue creature popped, releasing an eye-watering smell, and in its place once more was its regular woolly rump. The creature poked its head around the teapot. Their eyes met, and the little thing tilted its head on its side, as if it was thinking. Nine frowned, her grasp loosening on the handle of the net. The creature gave two quick sniffs in Nine's direction, and another in the direction of the teapot — and then bolted out of the bedroom door.

Nine gave a frustrated sigh and pulled herself out from the shadows. She sat back on her heels and looked around again at her mother's room. She wasn't sure who was the more astounded — her or

Flabberghast – when she had realised that her mother had once travelled with the House, and that the doorstep Nine vaguely remembered being left on with no more than a music box had not been a workhouse, or any old doorstep, but the House at the Edge of Magic. That had been before Pockets, the whiskery old gang-master, had stolen her away to be one of his pickpocketing thieflings, of course. It all seemed a lifetime ago...

"You had it all worked out for me, Ma," Nine whispered to herself. "Why did it all go wrong?" Her heart burned to know what had happened.

She had asked Flabberghast so many questions. Some he had answered, some he had avoided. He had met her ma when she was selling flowers on the street, in the mortal world. He had walked past and had an atrocious bout of sneezing. When her ma had passed him a handkerchief, an unexpected friendship had grown quickly between them.

The wizard's eyes had sparkled, all silvery and soft, when he spoke of the adventures they had shared. When Nine had asked why her ma had left, though, his eyes became dull and sad.

"People leave," he had said sharply. "They always do in the end." And he had refused to say any more.

Nine looked at the book that rested on her ma's bed. The golden letters of the title spelled out the title of her own favourite book, the one she always used to borrow from the library back home with Mr Downes, the best librarian in the world. *The Mystery of Wolven Moor.* Nine opened the front cover and traced her fingers over the handwritten name inside. Her ma's name. *Eliza.*

Nine peered again under the bed. Her ma's belongings. Things her ma would actually have touched. She lay down on her stomach again, reached for the fishing net and scooped up the teapot that the blue woolly creature had sniffed at. She brought the net out from under the bed and sat, resting against the iron bedframe. She looked at the delicate white china, decorated with golden stars. Nine stroked it thoughtfully. Had her mother made strawberry tea – the Finest Tea in All the Realms – in this very teapot? Why was it stuffed right underneath the bed? She lifted up the lid, peered inside ... and frowned

Inside were six pieces of ripped parchment. Nine reached into the teapot and pulled out the fragments. She turned them over in her hands. They had nothing written on them ... just pieces of plain parchment.

"Then … why rip it up?" Nine murmured aloud to the empty room. She rearranged the pieces, fitting them together to form the sheet of parchment. As she slotted the last one into place, her heart skipped a beat. Words appeared in spidery handwriting across the torn fragments:

Received with thanks,
The SAFEKEEPER

There was a sharp KNOCKITY-KNOCK on the bedroom door.

Nine jumped – and as she did so, her hand brushed one corner of the torn parchment, dislodging it from the other pieces. Nine stared at the parchment as the letters swiftly vanished from view. She hastily grabbed the pieces and stuffed them back inside the teapot.

Flabberghast's face peeped round the door, framed by his auburn curls poking out from his pointy, indigo hat.

"Madam? Ah! There you are," he said, drumming his fingers on the door. He stepped into the room. A silvery light sparkled in his ancient blue eyes as he glanced around. "She was quite … remarkable. A pity indeed that…"

18

The sparkle in his eyes faded instantly.

"What?" said Nine softly. She had to tread carefully. Her keen eyes watched him, searching for clues. "Come on. What are you not telling me?"

Flabberghast shrugged and his eyes looked sadder than before. "I suppose everyone has secrets, do they not?"

Nine said nothing, but the image of the torn parchment burned in her mind so strongly she felt Flabberghast would surely see it. She moved her hand slightly in front of the teapot.

What if the torn parchment was a secret Ma had kept from Flabberghast? Should I keep it? Should I say? Should I trust him—?

Flabberghast cleared his throat and brushed down his indigo pyjamas. "Although it was certainly no secret that she was fond of that wretched puffscuttler. The creatures live for decades."

Nine caught the whiff of something earthy and peppery in the air and her heart sank.

Oh, no...

"I bring warning," said Flabberghast, uneasily. "Eric is attempting to make up for your stolen breakfast by cooking you some pancakes."

Nine's shoulders slumped at the thought of the

grey, lumpy, bone-filled pancakes that the dear housekeeper troll was preparing. "And you didn't talk him out of it?"

"Well, Madam, you know what he's like," said Flabberghast. "He was so pleased to help. And he's..." The wizard grimaced. "He's adding a new ingredient."

Nine sighed. Eric was undoubtedly the best troll and the worst cook she had ever met in her life.

"Your sister has a lot to answer for. I can't believe she left all his recipe books translated into Dwarvish. We broke the curse on the House fair and square," Nine grumbled.

"Yes, well, I do not think *fairness* is my sister's strongest feature."

"But she *is* clever," said Nine, knowing it would annoy the wizard.

"What she is," Flabberghast said, "is a night-mare."

Nine felt the teapot, cool against her slightly sweating palm. Flabberghast hadn't recognised the teapot beside her. She was becoming increasingly convinced her ma hadn't trusted Flabberghast with whatever this secret was. So perhaps *she* shouldn't trust him with it, either.

"Madam?" asked Flabberghast, looking at her with a mixture of curiosity and nervousness. "You're not … *thinking* again, are you?"

"Well, one of us has to," Nine retorted. She pushed aside the guilt and the doubt, and picked up her satchel. Then she walked towards the door and grabbed Flabberghast by the sleeve.

"Madam?" said Flabberghast as she dragged him towards the rickety staircase.

"If *I* have to eat the bone pancakes, then *you're* going to as well."

And she marched him back down the plum-carpeted staircase, towards the strange, peppery, earthy smell, deliberately ignoring the flash of smug blue wool she could see out of the corner of her eye.

CHAPTER 2

As Nine and Flabberghast made their way downstairs, Nine heard the voices of her odd (and increasing) collection of housemates floating up from the kitchen.

"How much longer will this flamin' journey take?" grumbled Dr Spoon, who was surely the grumpiest and fiercest wooden spoon in the history of kitchen utensils.

"Flabby lost," came Eric's voice. It was followed by the ominous sound of a bone-pancake-laden plate being plonked on the kitchen table.

"For the last time, it's FLABB-ER-GHAST," Flabberghast protested loudly over Nine's shoulder as they came through the kitchen door. "Three syllables,

Eric. Please do keep trying. And I was not lost, I merely chose a creative way to reach our destination."

"Very creative," said Nine. "Going backwards was a real stroke of genius."

Flabberghast huffed. "It wasn't backwards. It was just ... not entirely forwards. That is very different."

Nine walked across the kitchen, putting some distance between herself and the squabble. The room was filled with cupboards of all different sizes. There was an archway with a locked wooden door on the right-hand wall, which led to the crypt housing Flabberghast's relatives, who were (somewhat unnervingly) only Sometimes Dead.

Beside the doorway was a tall hatstand and a bucket that caught orange slime, which dripped in large splats from the ceiling. On the left-hand side was a crockery-filled dresser and a large bricked fireplace with an ominously bubbling cauldron suspended above it. Next to it stood Eric the troll. He looked like a cross between a walrus and a tree trunk, with big, yellow eyes, and a ropey tail dangling behind him. He wore an apron, with a feather duster tucked into the strap.

Nine sat down and hooked her satchel over the back of the chair. She looked at her companion, Bonehead, the gloomy skeleton who up until recently had lived in a closet in the House under somewhat mysterious circumstances. Bonehead was looking suspiciously at the plate of grey, soggy pancakes steaming on the table in front of them, seeming rather grateful that he didn't need to eat.

"Bonehead!" hissed Nine to the skeleton, glancing over her shoulder at Flabberghast, who had joined the troll at the cauldron. She put a finger to her lips. "Who is the Safekeeper?"

"The Safekeeper? The one in Beyond?" whispered Bonehead, without moving his jaw. "Oooh, now, you don't want to be talking about him."

"Why not?" Nine whispered back. "Who is he?"

Dr Spoon was pacing around the kitchen on his spindly little legs, his moustache twitching with frustration. At the sight of their muttering, however, he bounded over to the table and leapt over the plate of pancakes. He stood in front of Nine on the table, frowning so his bushy, ginger eyebrows met in the middle, and narrowed his eyes at Nine. "What the devil are you up to now, lass?"

"Nothing! Nothing," said Nine.

Flabberghast headed back towards the table, and Nine, Bonehead and Spoon moved hastily apart. "Matters are worse than I thought," the wizard muttered, leaning on the table and lowering his voice. "I believe Eric is now attempting porridge."

Spoon groaned and put his face in his little hands.

"When we get to Beyond, all shall be well. He can buy a new cookbook. There's an … interesting bookshop there," said Flabberghast.

"Interesting?" said Nine suspiciously, who was getting to know the real meaning of words in the magical world. "Interesting as in fascinating, or interesting as in it's-going-to-try-to-kill-us?"

Flabberghast waved a hand dismissively. "Who knows, Madam! One or the other. Possibly both. Do not forget, we were trapped in the House for three years. A great deal can happen in three years."

"I tell you what's *not* happened in three years, lad," said Spoon, "and that's discovering the formula to make gold. I need my partner, Professor Dish, to put the formula together. We owe that formula, and our heads will roll if we don't deliver."

Flabberghast raised his hands in surrender. "I appreciate there has been a slight delay—"

"Three years trapped in a shrunken, cursed house, lad!"

"We are heading to Beyond as swiftly as possible, Dr Spoon—"

"Now we've finished going Not Entirely Forwards," muttered Nine.

"I would never have hitched a ride if I had known," grumbled Spoon. "We only split up because we were running out of time to deliver the gold and the flamin' formula wouldn't work! We were so close but we are still missing the ingredient that activates it!"

"Activates it?" said Nine.

Spoon seemed thrown for a moment. "It's a … technical term. We thought searching for it in different directions would work. I just hope Dish did nae end up trapped in a flamin' House, too!"

Flabberghast squirmed a little. "Dr Spoon, we will find Professor Dish with utmost urgency. The Asking Stone at the Tower at the End of Time cannot lie. If it told us the Professor was in Beyond, then she must be there."

Spoon hopped onto Flabberghast's shoulder and tugged a handful of the wizard's auburn curls. "And the Stone didn't just tell *us* that news, did it? That turnip-head of a wizard, Gazillion the Unstoppable, also asked the Stone where Dish was."

"That *was* odd. Why do you think Gazillion was interested?" said Nine.

"I told you, Madam, I do not know!" said Flabberghast.

"And at the Hopscotch Championship, why was he whispering to your aunt – that Ophidia the Unpredictable?" asked Nine.

"I do not know!"

"It must be something to do with Professor Dish, or why would Ophidia disappear in such a hurry?"

"MADAM! I DO NOT KNOW!" Flabberghast cried in exasperation. "We shall just have to hope we do not bump into either of them in Beyond."

"Tell you what *I* don't know, lad," grumbled Spoon, "and that's what you keep under that pointy hat, because I'm flamin' sure it isn't a brain!" Flabberghast gave an indignant huff.

Bonehead wiggled his skeleton fingers excitedly. "Well, it's all rather intriguing, if you ask me," he boomed. "Not that anyone does ask you when you're dead."

Eric trundled over and, with a wonky-tusky smile, plonked a large tureen of porridge on the table. Nine watched as green bubbles rose to the surface and popped with a deeply unpleasant smell. Bonehead followed her gaze.

"Of course, being dead does have its advantages," the skeleton added.

Suddenly, Nine felt a familiar strange feeling, like her brain was being sucked down through her body and out through her feet. She clutched the kitchen table, feeling sick and dizzy.

"Brace yourself, everyone!" cried Flabberghast. "We're landing!"

"Ooh," said Bonehead. "Here we go. Hold on to your skulls!"

Everything was moving too fast, hurtling in a direction Nine didn't understand but was quite possibly down, at a ridiculously fast pace. She closed her eyes until there was a little THUD.

And the dizziness stopped.

Spoon jumped down from Flabberghast's shoulder. "We find Dish, we leave," he said, skittering towards the front door, beckoning the others to follow.

Nine picked up her satchel and poked her head through the strap, swinging it across her body. She dashed towards Eric, grabbed his long-nailed hand and pulled him towards the front door, feeling a small tingle of excitement in her stomach. Bonehead followed them.

"Ah, yes. We shall indeed leave… After we have completed our shopping task, that is," Flabberghast said quietly, as he slid between Spoon and the front door.

"Shopping task?" asked Nine.

"It's the law of Beyond," said Flabberghast, shrugging. "It was the idea of Affluenza the Stonkingly Ridiculously Wealthy when she was chair of the Beyond Committee. Every household must buy or trade something from every single shop – otherwise your house is not permitted to leave."

"Not permitted? Or else what?" said Nine.

"If you attempt a counter-spell to sneak off early, then it rather regretfully backfires and your house is stuck to the ground for a month. The parking charges are unbelievable! And even worse, anyone who is caught must clean out the public chamber pots every single day." Flabberghast pulled a face.

Nine couldn't help a little smile. "You tried to sneak off early once, didn't you?"

"I refuse to discuss the matter," said Flabberghast and sniffed haughtily.

"Eric shop!" said Eric, pulling the front pocket of his apron inside out. "Sweets gone! Buy sweets!"

"Indeed," said Flabberghast. "You take the sweet shop, Eric." He cleared his throat. "And, um, might

I suggest you visit the bookshop? Perhaps you'd like to find a few new recipes?"

As Eric pulled out his feather duster from his apron strap and leaned it against the wall, the wizard moved towards an umbrella stand by the door and stretched out his hand. "Cloak."

A blue arm shot out of the umbrella stand, holding an indigo, star-speckled cloak in its blue fingers. Nine stared at it. She had always wondered who – or what – that arm actually belonged to. There were still so many questions about this mysterious, magical House.

"Blimey, your House is a bit rusty with the ol' landing, ain't it?" said a gruff female voice from behind.

Nine turned to see the newest member of the household: Cascadia Spout, the gargoyle. She waddled down the stairs towards them. She was a mottled grey colour, with small wings, chunky, short legs and a bulbous nose.

"Found me room," said Cas. "Nice little spot at the top of a tower. Even got me own ledge outside the window."

Flabberghast reached deep inside his cloak and pulled out a handful of little purple drawstring bags which jingled hopefully.

"Marvellous. Now, listen. You will all require these," he said, handing a bag to Eric, Spoon, Nine and Cas.

Nine's eyes lit up as she stared at the bag in her hand. She squidged it around, listening to the dull clanking of coins. What she would have given to hold a bag like this when she was a pickpocket in her days before the House! She tucked the bag inside her satchel.

"The priority, of course, is to discover the whereabouts of Professor Dish and rescue her. We must make enquiries carefully. I do not know the involvement of my aunt, Ophidia the Unpredictable, though I'm very sure we want to find that dish before she does, if indeed that is what she seeks."

"We gathered that," said Nine.

"And she's not called the Unpredictable for nothing!"

"We gathered that, too," said Nine.

"I dearly hope I can find an answer to restoring my magic, but we must also decide who is going to buy what from where," continued Flabberghast. "The last thing we want to do once we've found the Professor is be trapped here because everybody bought sweets, and nobody bought socks!"

"Socks?" boomed Bonehead joyfully. "I haven't

worn socks for years. Of course, nobody thinks about your feet when you're dead. Your toes all chilly in winter…"

"Good!" exploded Spoon, in a voice that suggested there was nothing good about it at all. "Now do you think we could actually get on with finding Professor Dish? That's what we're here for! Not flamin' socks!"

"And I wholeheartedly agree," said Flabberghast, dropping a little purple purse of coins into the skeleton's bony hand. Then he moved sharply to the front door and cleared his throat. "Friends!" he announced dramatically, flinging open the front door. "Welcome to Beyond."

CHAPTER 3

The first thing Nine noticed was that there was a tiny wicker shopping basket the size of a matchbox floating outside the door, level with her eyes. Its little handles were flopped by its sides.

The second thing she noticed were the magnificent houses that surrounded them closely everywhere. It was like they had landed in the middle of a crowded street, except there was hardly any space between the buildings.

Some were more like overbearing castles, built of black or grey stone, with tall towers and arrow-slit windows – and some even had a drawbridge. Others seemed to be built of smooth, polished marble – gleaming and spotless and twice as tall as the House

33

at the Edge of Magic. All of them had turrets and towers and windows … and looked a darn sight better than their House.

Nine quickly glanced back at their own eleven-storeyed home – rickety, wonky, with rooms jutting out everywhere, like they'd been slapped on in a hurry by an architect who was blindfolded and probably half-asleep.

Still, she wasn't sure she'd change it.

"This is the House Park," explained Flabberghast, standing next to Nine. "Everybody always polishes up their houses before they arrive."

"Almost everyone," said Nine. She glanced up at the ramshackle House.

"Our House is magnificent just the way it is," said Flabberghast, lifting his nose further into the air. A wonky roof tile fell off and dropped by Nine's feet.

Flabberghast stared at the tile and sighed defeatedly. He pushed a couple of dark brown coins into Nine's hands. "These are called yonders, Madam. Would you be so good as to arrange the parking ticket? The meter's over there." He waved his arm in the direction of what looked like a bronze statue of a dragon sitting on top of a stone pedestal. "And don't annoy it, or it'll give us a fine."

"How do you annoy a parking meter?"

"I'm sure you'll find a way, Madam," Flabberghast said curtly.

Nine snorted. The floating basket stayed hovering at the front door as Nine began to move towards the meter, when Cascadia crashed into the back of Nine's knees.

"Blimey," she said, pointing with a stony hand towards a particularly austere-looking black castle with jagged spearheads lining the turrets. "I spent years of me life sittin' on that one!" Cas rubbed her stony backside and seemed to wince at the memory. "I tell you, I don't fancy bumpin' into Malissa the Unnecessarily Spiteful."

"Can't think why," said Nine. "She sounds lovely."

"Hurry up, lass!" bellowed Spoon from behind.

"All right!" said Nine, marching on towards the parking meter. The little bronze dragon statue was half as tall as Nine, but sitting on the pedestal brought it up to her eye height. It was sitting on its hind legs, its tail wrapped around itself, and had its eyes firmly shut. A black cloak rested on the ground behind it. Nine wondered how exactly she was meant to pay for parking. Tentatively, she reached out a finger and prodded it. The bronze statue opened one eye.

"No," said the dragon. "It's too busy. I want a nap."

"But I need a ticket," said Nine, prodding the statue in the ribs.

"Stop it! That tickles! I can fine you, you know."

Nine sighed. "I just want a parking ticket."

"And I just want a nap. My belly's absolutely full. Makes me all sleepy." The dragon yawned.

"BUT I NEED A TICKET." She prodded the statue again.

"All right, all right! One last ticket! And, in return, you pick up that cloak on the ground there and put it over me. It's blown off again."

"Fine," said Nine.

"Coins," said the dragon, opening its mouth.

Cautiously, Nine dropped the yonders Flabberghast had given her inside the creature's mouth. It swallowed them with a big gulp, followed by a clinking of metal as the coins landed in its stomach.

The dragon squirmed a little, as if it was trying to get in the right position for something.

"Where's my ticket?" said Nine.

"Hang on, it's coming," said the dragon. "It's coming…" It squirmed again, then opened its stony jaws and let out an enormous burp. As it did so, a little ticket came flying out of its mouth. Nine grabbed it quickly before it fell to the ground.

"That's disgusting," said Nine, holding the ticket with the tips of her fingers.

The dragon shrugged. "That's business. Cloak."

Nine picked up the cloak and threw it over the dragon. It had a handwritten sign on it saying OUT OF ORDER. Underneath the cloth, the dragon immediately began to snore.

Nine marched back to Flabberghast, who tucked the ticket under the doorknocker before turning back to her with a grin. "Now we can… Ohhhhhh dear." His grin fell.

"Now what?" roared Spoon, jumping up and down on the spot with his spindly legs.

"That house over there," said Flabberghast. "It belongs to my Aunt Ophidia. She's here!"

Nine followed his gaze to a narrow, overbearing house built of blood-red granite. Three tall, spiky towers with narrow windows made the house look like a rather unfriendly trident.

"Then there's even less time to lose!" said Spoon. "I tell you, lad, if I had my sword, it would be poking your backside right now. LET'S FIND PROFESSOR DISH."

Flabberghast nodded. "I suggest finding you a new sword would be a good starting point. I rather think it might come in handy. And I must visit the apothecary to see if there are any solutions to restoring my magic."

"If we split up, we'll be quicker," said Nine. "We can ask after Dish and get something from each shop as we go."

"Agreed," said Flabberghast. They moved swiftly through the House Park, marching through alleys made between the towering, turreted houses – the little shopping basket following close behind. "Dr Spoon, you come with me, and I shall show you the blacksmith. She's based near the apothecary, the Cloaks & Jokes shop, and the Finest Tea Shop in All the Realms, so we shall start there and then go on to Locke Street."

"What about me?" said Nine.

"Eric sweets?" rumbled the troll, looking at Nine with hopeful yellow eyes. "Lady come?"

Nine smiled at the thought of a sweet shop, particularly one with a delighted troll in it. "Expect I could manage that." But as much as she wanted to go, her mind was turning to the Safekeeper. Who was he? Where was he? And what was he keeping safe for her ma?

"Splendid," said Flabberghast, crashing through her thoughts. "And, Madam, you and Eric cover the candlemakers, the Secret Shop of Secrets and the bookshop." He pointed at Nine, his tone suddenly serious. "And whatever you do, Madam, do *not* buy any candle that speaks, regardless of what it tells you."

"Speaks? Candles don't speak!"

"Precisely," said Flabberghast, as if the matter was closed.

"I shall take the sock shop," said Bonehead. He wiggled his bony fingers excitedly.

"And, Miss Spout, if you would be so good as to accompany him to Harkdark Street, Sevenstar Lane and Yonder Alley. I suggest you consider buying something like a hat and a toilet brush."

"Not that we'll ever catch the toilet," muttered Nine. "Why *does* it wander about?"

"Who knows?" said Flabberghast. "I'm not even entirely sure what it's doing in the House."

"And what do I want a hat for?" blurted out Cas, as they scurried down between a square, white-marbled house with balconies and a rather tall, narrow stone tower.

"So we may leave," said Flabberghast tightly. "And whatever you do, don't buy a dreadful one with flowers. They irritate my nasal lining. Ah, here we are."

Nine's eyes opened wide as she stared at Beyond. There were dozens of buildings in clusters together, separated by little alleyways with cobbled stones. But they weren't normal-looking buildings. They were brightly coloured – and shaped like items. Nine could see a black boot-shaped building with windows; a bottle-shaped building made of green glass with pink smoke wisping out of its top; a transparent hourglass-shaped shop which suddenly flipped over, sending all its customers sliding through the funnel back to the bottom; and a tall white building with a flame roaring on its roof towering in the distance.

Between all these marvellous shops, hundreds of witches and wizards of all ages bustled around in a glorious swirl of colourful cloaks. There were other magical folk, too – Nine was sure she spotted a griffin disappearing into the hourglass – and everyone was followed by a floating shopping basket of various sizes, stacked high with magical things.

"Be mindful when you enquire after Professor Dish," said Flabberghast, interrupting Nine's amazement. "You never know who is listening and we do not wish to bump into my Aunt Ophidia. She will be here shopping in every single shop, just like us. We shall take the basket first, and meet here again within the hour and exchange our news. Good luck!" He nodded curtly and marched off down an alley on the right with Spoon skittering along beside him.

Bonehead began to stride away, the basket floating behind, but Nine grabbed his bony arm and pulled him back. "Wait! The Safekeeper!" she hissed. "You said he was in Beyond. Who is he? What does he do?"

"I thought that would be obvious. I have no brain and it's even obvious to me." Bonehead leaned towards her. "He keeps things safe, of course." He lowered his voice ominously. "For a price. Things that are important – yet dangerous. Rather like him, I suppose."

Nine frowned. Why would her ma have something dangerous? "Where can I find him?"

"Haven't the foggiest. He moves around, from location to location. That's how he keeps things safe. But I wouldn't find him if I were you. Trouble awaits, without a doubt." Nine sighed in frustration as Bonehead leaned away from her again and wiggled his fingers. "I am rather excited about the socks. They might have fluffy ones." He strode away down the street.

Cas looked at Nine. "Course, us gargoyles know a thing or two what we're not meant to," she said. "Very good at sittin' still and hearin' stuff and not bein' noticed. I'll make enquiries about your Safekeeper."

"Really? Thank you, Cas," said Nine.

"Come, Cascadia!" the skeleton boomed over his bony shoulder. "You must buy a hat."

"Me head's made of stone! Not exactly a problem if it gets wet, is it?" Cas muttered, but she scuttled after him, trying determinedly to keep up on her short, stony legs.

Nine turned to Eric after the others disappeared into the crowd. He had pulled his tail forwards and was wringing it.

"Keeper? Danger things?" said the troll, with big, worried eyes.

"Don't worry about it," Nine said. She gave him a smile. "Eric sweets?"

Eric gave a wonky-tusky smile, but his eyes still looked worried. "Eric sweets."

He trundled away over the cobbled stones and Nine followed behind.

Important and dangerous.

What *had* her ma left behind?

CHAPTER 4

He pointed his long fingernail towards a shop that was bulbous in shape, with two side extensions like the twisted corners of a sweet wrapper. The building was garishly painted with wide stripes of blue, red, brown, green and orange. It looked like someone was still deciding which colour it should be – or what flavour. There was a little skip in the troll's step as he clapped his huge, bark-like hands together and headed for the round shop door in the middle.

"How do we get in? There's no door handle," said Nine. She went to peer through the tiny sweet-shaped window in the door...

Suddenly, an O-shaped mouth opened up in the middle of the door and sucked them inside with a noisy, slurping sound. Nine had barely regained her balance as the door-mouth closed back up behind them and made a satisfied "mmmmm". Nine's eyes widened as she looked around.

Every spare inch of every wall was lined with shelves of tall jars, packed full of sweets of every colour and shape. A blue-and-white striped counter stood in front of one of the walls, packed with more jars of sweets, and behind it stood a bald, older wizard in a blue robe, with a silvery beard so bushy it was twice as wide as his face. He gave a big grin, showing a flash of shiny too-white teeth that couldn't possibly be real.

"Customers! Customers! Welcome, friends!" said the wizard, dashing out from behind the counter more quickly than was strictly necessary, his robe flapping around him. "Aniseed the Regretfully Toothless at your service!" He thrust a pink-and-white striped paper bag into Nine's hands, and another into Eric's, whose palms were already outstretched and waiting.

Nine froze awkwardly as the wizard darted around them, peering over their shoulders, then rushing in front of them and staring at their eyes. Eric just stood there grinning, his hands clasping his sweet bag happily.

"Hmm, let me think! Let me think! The perfect sweet for you…" The wizard examined Eric thoughtfully, then closed his bright, blue eyes and frowned in concentration, with his fingertips to his temples.

Eric jiggled on the spot, his wide eyes glancing hopefully at the jar of brown-and-white stripy sweets on a high shelf.

"Is he trying to read your mind?" Nine said to the troll, feeling her shoulders tense. "Can he *do* that?"

One of the wizard's eyes peeped open a crack and followed Eric's gaze. Then both of his eyes flew open.

"Of course, of course! I have just the one!" He twisted his wrist, and there was a crackle of pale blue lightning from his fingers. Nine jumped as the lid went spinning off the jar of brown-and-white stripy sweets. Another wrist-twist and a torrent of sweets flew out of the jar, arching down towards the paper bag in Eric's grasp.

Nine eyed the wizard suspiciously but the troll gave a squeak of joy. "Best sweet! Best sweet! Eric love!"

"Of course you do, my friend! Of course! Have more, have more!" Aniseed the Regretfully Toothless grabbed another stripy bag from the counter.

Eric nodded excitedly, but Nine moved slightly in front of him.

"We have other shops to visit, thank you very much," she said sharply.

"Of course, of course!" said the wizard, still flashing his too-white-to-be-real teeth, although Nine's sharp, pickpocket sight noticed how his left eye narrowed and twitched very slightly. "And what shall you have, I wonder? Let me think, let me think!" The wizard and his beard swept directly in front of Nine, his blue eyes staring deeply into Nine's brown ones.

"No-no. You're not reading *my* mind," she said firmly, staring back at the wizard.

The wizard screwed his eyes shut, frowned in concentration and put his fingertips to his temples.

"Let me think... The perfect sweet! The perfect sweet!"

Just in case Aniseed the Regretfully Toothless really was reading her mind, Nine glanced at every jar she could see. They all looked wonderful and exciting. She wanted them all and this made her feel smug. She looked back at the wizard just in time to see a peeking eye slam shut, then both eyes fly open.

"Everything! Everything for you!"

Nine rolled her eyes.

There were twists of the wrist, crackles of blue

lightning, then rainbow streams of sweets arched down from all the jars, fighting and shoving their way into the pink-and-white bag in Nine's hand.

"Lady lucky!" said Eric next to her, still grinning.

The last few sweets tussled their way into Nine's bag. Nine jumped as another crackle made the top of her paper bag twist at the corners and roll itself down, safely sealed. The rainbow streams of sweets sped back to their jars and all the lids quickly twisted back on. There was silence and stillness in the shop. Except for the wizard, who rubbed his hands together.

"Come, come, my friends," he said joyfully. "That will be two yonders each!"

Nine glared at Aniseed the Regretfully Toothless suspiciously. She opened her satchel, put in the bag of sweets and fumbled around for the little purse Flabberghast had given her. As she did, her fingertips brushed her precious music box and ... something else. Something soft. She frowned for a second, then remembered. It was a little velvet pouch she had pickpocketed from another witch when they had been to the Hopscotch Championship. Her fingers closed around it briefly. The miniature sapphire skull that had once been inside it had been lost at the championship, but the little pouch still held a tiny bottle with blue smoke swirling inside and a couple of coins.

"Thank you, thank you!" the wizard chortled as Eric handed over his coins, breaking Nine's thoughts. Nine pulled out the purse, took out two dark brown yonders and dropped them into the wizard's hand.

"Thank you, thank you! Enjoy your sweets!"

"Eric will! Love sweets!" The troll grinned as he trundled towards the door.

"Wait! We need to ask about Dish!" Nine whispered to him, then turned to look at the wizard warily. "Before we go, I have a question. We're looking for a dish—"

The wizard's jovial expression dropped suddenly. His face darkened as he stared at Nine. "I have not seen her, I have not heard of her," he said in a low voice. "And if I had, I would not speak of it. Ophidia the Unpredictable is not a foe I would choose."

Nine felt prickles of unease run up and down her back. "I didn't mention Ophidia the Unpredictable. You *do* know of Professor Dish! Where is she?"

There was a flash of panic in Aniseed's eyes. "Come again soon, friends!" said the wizard in an overly loud and merry voice. He put one hand on the counter and leapt over it, his beard swishing wildly.

He pushed urgently at Nine's back, steering her to the round door, which Eric now held open. He bundled them both out, flashing them one last, glittering smile. "You are most welcome any time! Any time!"

And he slammed the door in their faces and flipped the door sign to CLOSED, as a slatted wooden blind unrolled swiftly down the window.

Eric's happy face fell, and he looked at Nine with worried, yellow eyes. "Trouble?" he said in a wobbly voice. He pulled out a sweet and pushed it into Nine's hand.

"Trouble," Nine said to him. "I don't think finding Dish is going to be as easy as we thought. But we must find her before Ophidia the Unpredictable does. Let's try the candlemaker's. Come on."

CHAPTER
5

The towering candlemaker's shop was not hard to spot. There was a distant glow of flame atop the tall white building coming from an alleyway between the sweet shop and a huge, multi-storeyed building shaped like a giant – and slightly wonky – pointy hat.

Nine felt odd as she turned down the passage towards the bright glow. It wasn't that long ago that she would have run down an alleyway such as this, having pickpocketed someone at the local market. Now here she was, strolling down one, with a troll for company and a satchel full of sweets, looking for a dish who knew how to turn things into gold.

Was this what her mother had imagined life would be like for Nine when she had left her at the

50

House at the Edge of Magic? Nine knew so little about her ma...

RECEIVED WITH THANKS, THE SAFEKEEPER.

The words danced around in Nine's mind as she walked towards the bright glow, which seemed to come from the left-hand side at the end of the alley. What *had* her mother given the Safekeeper, and could it answer some of her questions?

Nine's thoughts were suddenly interrupted by her pickpocket senses tingling. Something was wrong. Someone – or something? – was following them.

She slowed her step, sharpened her ears – but the only sound was the long-toenailed feet of Eric and her own, slightly faster, heartbeat. Still, as she walked further down the alleyway, the feeling grew stronger and stronger. Nine's breathing became shallower and faster... Muscles tensed, ready for action. Someone – something – behind her. BEHIND HER—

Unable to bear it any longer, Nine whirled around, fists clenched.

An empty alleyway.

No one.

Nothing.

Having had experience of wandering the realms of magic, Nine had learned to no longer trust her eyes, but to trust her instincts – instincts which were screaming that there was, without question, someone behind them. Someone who had no intention of being seen.

And that, Nine had to admit, was almost certainly a problem.

Her heart thumping, Nine grabbed Eric's bark-like arm and speedily marched on down the alleyway towards the glow of the candlemaker's shop. Letting out a long breath, Nine reached the end of the alleyway and turned left. There stood a tall, thin and round windowless building made of curved, white-washed bricks. The golden, fiery beacon at its top flickered in the slight breeze. A little sign creaked on a bracket sticking out of the wall: Wax & Wicks.

Nine turned and looked at the alley one last time. "I know you're there," she said, trying to keep the fear out of her voice. "And you don't scare me."

"Scares Eric."

She pulled the troll towards the shop's narrow white door, yanked the door open and tried to shove Eric inside. But broad trolls and narrow doorways were never going to be a great match. Nine pushed and shoved him until, with a satisfying *pop*, Eric landed in the shop. Nine dashed in after him and slammed the door behind her.

As she did, she realised she was standing in pitch darkness. She sighed loudly. Why couldn't things ever be normal?

"Not like," whimpered Eric. There was the sound of long-toenailed shuffling, and then the feeling of a long-toenailed foot squashing her own shoe.

"You need to be a bit braver," Nine whispered. She gently steered Eric away from her foot, but not too far away. Coming from the daylight of Beyond to the blackness of the shop, Nine's eyes were struggling to see anything. And, she had to admit, she didn't like it at all.

There was a sudden WHOOSH as a tiny yellow flame burst into life a little way ahead of them. And another a little way above it. And another...

Nine stared at the flames as dozens lit up, going higher and higher as if they were sitting on the rungs of a ladder or—

"A staircase," Nine breathed. "I suppose we go up."

She moved warily through the gloom, holding tight to Eric's hand. He squeezed tightly back. As she climbed up the barely visible, creaking steps, each candle seemed to whisper, "Pick *me*! Pick *me*!"

"Candle speak!" Eric said, and even in the dark, Nine could sense his wibbly, downturned mouth.

"Don't worry," Nine whispered back. "I won't touch them."

As Nine reached the top of the staircase, with the glow of the tiny candles behind her, she was once more standing in darkness. She tightened her grip on Eric's rough fingers. "Now what?" she whispered.

WHOOSH!

There was a blaze of light as dozens of candles suddenly burst into flame. There were flames of every colour – even rainbow-coloured – revealing candles of every shape and size. Some were squat and wide; some were elaborately carved, like fountains solidified in wax. Some were well burned and standing in saucers on spindly-legged stools; others were perched on tiny shelves on the walls.

There were tall candles in candlestick holders, and even a couple of candle-lit chandeliers hanging from the ceiling. The flickering lights threw up threatening shadows of more candles all over the high, round walls.

Nine looked at Eric. There was a chilly, un-welcome feel in the air, which was odd when sur-rounded by so much light and flame. Nine looked around her.

No sign of anyone.

A chubby red candle with golden swirls stood within reach. "I suppose … we just take one?" she asked, her fingers twitching towards it.

Suddenly every flickering flame went out, plunging them into darkness once more. Nine didn't know whether to gasp or sigh, but, before she could decide, there was another WHOOSH of air and light as the candles all burst into life.

Nine jumped.

An extremely tall witch stood on the other side of the room. She wore a black cloak and had thin, black hair pulled back in a tight bun. Her eyes were narrowed, and she had the expression of someone who'd been chewing on a dead slug for a fortnight.

"Hello," said Nine, feeling decidedly short. "We'd like to buy a candle."

The tall witch stared at them with all the warmth of a frozen puddle. She tutted noisily – and the flames extinguished again.

"Could you stop *doing* that?"

"No like," said Eric as he stepped on Nine's foot again.

WHOOSH! The flames lit up once more and the shopkeeper was standing right in front of her.

"I dislike customers," she said. "Handling my stock. Disturbing my peace. I crave the darkness."

"I'd never have guessed," muttered Nine. She lifted her head to look defiantly into the shopkeeper's eyes.

"Just take this one," hissed the tall witch, thrusting a thin white candle into Nine's hands. "Take it! Now leave!"

Nine glanced at the candle in her hands. "But we haven't paid—"

"No charge. It's nothing but trouble anyway. Take the wretched thing. Now go."

Nine could feel another WHOOSH coming on. "Wait! I need to ask something. We're looking for a dish... A dish who can probably talk and—"

The flames, which had begun to dim, bounced into life again. Nine leapt out of her skin to see the tall witch towering above her, closer than before.

"Oh, *she* can talk!" growled the shopkeeper. "Moaned on and on about the candle I sold her last week and had the cheek to bring it back!" She bent over Nine, her dark eyes dancing with candle flames. "NOW. LEAVE!"

The candles extinguished and there was silence in the shop – silence, except for Nine huffing loudly. Then the little candles on the stairs below began lighting up one by one, as if ushering their customers out.

"Goodbye, goodbye," the candles whispered as Nine and Eric stepped tentatively down each stair.

"Bye bye," Eric replied.

"We weren't talking to *you* two," whispered one of the candles. The others seemed to stifle a giggle.

Nine had the familiar feeling of frustration and impending doom – candles giggling at her was probably not a great sign. She shoved the candle she'd been given into her satchel then reached in the darkness for Eric's hand. They stumbled their way back to the front door and stepped back out into the street.

The daylight burned Nine's eyes after spending so much time in the dark. But far worse than that was the instant feeling that she was still being watched...

She cast her keen pickpocket eyes around, but there was no sign of anyone – or anything – following her. As she turned to look down the passage between the hat shop and the sweet shop, she saw Bonehead walking past the entrance to the passage, wearing a pair of bright pink fluffy socks. He turned his head and gave Nine a stiff wave, followed by a happy little skip as he strode on towards a long, winding snake-shaped building, which led back from the street.

A second later, Cas scurried after him on her short legs, weaving through the other customers on the street. She was wearing an enormous pointy hat that rested on her shoulders, decorated with garish, oversized flowers. She paused for a moment, raising the brim of her hat with one finger. She looked at Nine, gave a wink and scurried on after the skeleton as they both entered the gaping, unhinged mouth of the snake and disappeared into the building.

Nine eyed it curiously. The only window seemed to be the snake's eye. Nine walked towards the building and read the bat-shaped sign on the wall: *Pest Shop*. She stood on tiptoe and peered through the eye-shaped windowpane.

Inside, in between all the bustling customers, Nine caught glimpses of cages and tanks of all sizes lining the long wall. She saw strange and marvellous creatures from miniature silver dragons to giant turquoise beetles. One small cage was covered in black cloth and had a thick, padlocked chain wound around it. Next to it, a glass tank housed a bright orange puff of smoke, which faded away … only to repuff a few seconds later. A sign on the wall read "Special Offer: DRAGON DROPPINGS 10% OFF!"

Who in their right mind would want dragon droppings?

"No window shopping!" hissed a serpentine voice from somewhere near by.

Nine leapt backwards to see an eyelid like a window shutter flash across the window, soon replaced by the unblinking eye-slit of a serpent.

"Fine," said Nine. "I'm not interested in pests. I have enough trouble with the ones already in my house." She glared at the eye, then made her way back to Eric. "Dish is definitely here somewhere. The shopkeepers know about her."

"How find?" said Eric, scratching his head with his long fingernail.

"That's the problem," said Nine, looking around at the hordes of wizards and witches busying along the cobbles, followed by their packed, floating baskets. "I have no idea."

Then a little giggle came from Nine's satchel, and a tiny voice piped up: "But *I* have."

CHAPTER 6

Nine froze and Eric clapped his long-nailed hands over his mouth. His eyes opened wide and he pointed at Nine's satchel.

"Candle speak! Candle speak!"

Nine swallowed hard, remembering Flabberghast's very specific warning *not* to get a talking candle. She peeled open the flap of her satchel cautiously and peered inside.

It was just a candle. Just a simple, normal—

"Boo!" said the flame, which briefly appeared at the end of the candle. The flame looked like a little face. It then burst into giggles – and extinguished, leaving a tiny black scorch mark inside the satchel.

Nine slammed down the flap of the satchel and

rubbed her hand over her eyes. The day was really not going well.

"Ooh, sweeties!" said a muffled voice from inside the bag.

"Don't you dare eat my sweets!" Nine hissed.

There was more giggling.

"Candle laugh!" wailed Eric.

"Yes, I know," Nine said irritably.

"Flabby warned!"

"Yes. I know."

"Big trouble!"

"YES! I KNOW!"

Eric reached hastily into his apron pocket, grabbed a large handful of boiled sweets and stuffed the lot into his mouth, making his cheeks bulge.

"I'm having words with this candle," Nine said. "Come on, we need somewhere quiet. Well, it *will* be quiet until this candle gets there."

She took Eric by the arm and led him over to what looked like a giant, flowery chamber pot with a row of doors along its front. A young witch dressed in a grey velvet cloak and a lopsided hat ran towards one of the closed doors and knocked on it urgently as she jiggled on the spot. Eric gave her a sympathetic look.

Nine and Eric ducked around the back, where above a pile of chipped old chamber pots, Nine noticed a torn and faded poster nailed to the wall. It was a picture of a cheeky-looking toilet – the toilet currently in *their* house, to be precise' – hopping away on its pedestal, followed by the words:

WANTED

RUNAWAY TOILET.

CHECK YOUR HOUSES.

REWARD OFFERED.

CONTACT VIA MESSAGE URN.

THANK YOU.

MAGENTA THE INCREASINGLY DESPERATE.

Nine rolled her eyes. Tempting as a reward might be, there were other things to focus on. She quickly peered around the building in case anyone was watching, but the coast was clear. Nine reached into her satchel, pulled out the candle and turned it over in her hands. It looked just like a normal candle. She leaned closer to it.

"Hello?" Nine whispered.

The flame burst into life once more. Nine jerked her head backwards, her heart thumping, holding it at arm's length. In the flame, a face appeared and blew a loud raspberry, its fiery tongue poking out. Then, as fast as it had appeared, the flame extinguished again.

Eric covered his eyes with his hands, then peeped through his fingernails.

"Right," said Nine firmly, using her best not-taking-any-nonsense-from-candles voice. "Unless you want me to take you right back to that candle shop, you'd better start being helpful."

A tiny flame with a sulky face appeared at the end of the candle. "Spoilsport."

"Now listen," Nine said, dropping her voice and bringing the candle close – but not *too* close – to her face. "We are looking for a dish: a walking, talking dish, who is conducting experiments. You said you knew something."

"Maybe."

Nine jabbed the candle with her finger. "Tell me."

"What's in it for me?"

Nine narrowed her eyes. "I won't tie a candle snuffer on your head."

"Rude." The candle pouted. "All I know is, she's doing all these strange experiments, long into the night. Needed some candles to work by. I was only being helpful, pointing out mistakes... Giving advice..." The candle sniffed and looked rather offended. "But some people are just *so* ungrateful..."

"Where is she?" said Nine, hope firing inside her.

"She brought me back to the shop, complaining that I was *distracting* her by talking so much. But that was just an excuse as the real reason was because I lit up and made her jump and drop that silver ball in her potion but it was only a *small* explosion and—"

"*Where is she?*" Nine growled through gritted teeth. She gave the candle a little shake. The flame on the top bobbed about in the air.

"All right, all right! Don't get your wickers in a twist. In the basement of the This-and-That Shop." The flame dimmed a little. "She needed a little of this, a little of that for her experiments, you see. So there, I've told you and been ever so helpful, so please don't take me back to Wax & Wicks. You won't believe how reeeeeally boring it is there."

Nine twisted her mouth and looked at Eric.

"Flabby warned," the troll said, wringing his tail.

The candle's eyes became big and doleful. "Pleeeeeeease."

Nine sighed and leaned closer to the candle again. "No one must ever know you're a talking candle, all right? Especially—"

"Ah, Madam!" came a voice behind them.

Nine's heart skipped a beat as she whirled around, keeping the candle behind her back. A jiggling Flabberghast and a sword-wielding Spoon were coming towards them, the shopping basket floating behind them, now larger in size and filled with a polka-dot cloak and a collection of colourful bottles that seemed to have muffled laughter stuck inside them.

Nine quickly turned her back to them and blew out the candle, which gave an indignant squeak. She threw it into her satchel and turned back to Flabberghast and Spoon.

"Just using the facilities," Flabberghast said, cloak flapping as he darted towards one of the doors in the giant chamber pot. "I fear I may have drunk one strawberry tea too many at the Finest Tea Shop in All the Realms!" He dashed inside, slamming the door behind him, the shopping basket skidding to a halt in front of the door. "I had to cheer myself up after the apothecary said she had no idea how to restore my powers—"

"Flabberghast, listen! Spoon!" Nine said to the chamber pot door. "Dish is in the basement of the This-and-That Shop!"

Spoon gave a whoop and leapt into the air, swishing his sword around wildly. "At last! Well done, lass!"

"Madam, such news! We must go at once!" came Flabberghast's muffled voice through the door, sounding relieved in more ways than one. "Well … one moment."

Soon they were trotting along behind Flabberghast once more, scurrying past a shop shaped like a doughnut that released the most entrancing smell. The wizard, however, showed no signs of slowing – not even for a snack.

"Now, take heed. My Aunt Ophidia the Unpredictable is here somewhere and, I fear, Gazillion the Unstoppable may be accompanying her. We do NOT wish to run into them."

"Oooh! We most certainly do not!" chirped a voice from Nine's satchel.

Flabberghast stopped abruptly, and Eric, Nine and Spoon all crashed into each other as they came to a halt, with the shopping basket at the rear shoving into Nine's back.

She gave her satchel a firm slap as Flabberghast turned around, looking at Nine with a frown.

"Are you quite all right, Madam?"

Nine cleared her throat. "Fine! Fine… My throat…"

Flabberghast gave a sharp if dubious nod.

They carried on through the winding streets, passing hordes of witches and wizards with shopping baskets floating behind. One wizard walked by with an orange, dragon-shaped bathing ring around his waist, humming happily to himself, and Nine turned her head to watch him walk by. Then a shot of cold hit her insides.

Because there in the distance, but still far too close for her liking, marched Ophidia the Unpredictable, with her unmistakable wild mop of curly white hair and her emerald cloak trailing along the ground. Behind her strutted Gazillion the Unstoppable (and recently unturnipped).

"Gazillion!" cried Nine, reaching forwards and tugging Flabberghast's star-speckled cloak.

The wizard gave a high-pitched squeak and dived down a little alley on the left. Nine and the others rushed after him, the shopping basket following at such speed that it couldn't stop in time and bonked Eric right on the head.

Nine peeped around and watched Ophidia and Gazillion walk by. The shopping basket peeped around too until Nine pushed it back.

She watched Gazillion suspiciously. The wizard's

blond hair still had a greenish tinge, and his face was still slightly mauve. He swished his mauve cloak around him arrogantly as he and Ophidia marched right through a group of witches, wizards and other magical folk, scattering them left and right.

"Do you suppose he's forgiven you yet for turning him into a turnip?" Nine whispered.

"I suspect Eric will speak in three-syllable words before that happens," muttered Flabberghast.

A large shopping basket floated behind Ophidia and Gazillion, full of a complete set of stacking cauldrons, a yellow baby dragon and a large pot plant with clam-like, toothy jaws at the end of a long stem, which snapped at everyone who passed.

Nine watched Ophidia point to another alleyway opposite the one they had leapt down. Gazillion nodded and headed in that direction, while Ophidia carried on down the main street. They had a look of urgency as they split up and hurried off, presumably rushing to gather all their items so they could leave Beyond.

It wasn't long before they both disappeared from view, and Nine felt herself let out a small sigh of relief. Creeping out from their spot in the alleyway, Nine turned her eyes back to the street – and found herself directly in front of the This-and-That Shop.

It was in the shape of the initials that made up its name, with two tall towers shaped like "T"s either side of a timber-framed "A" in the middle. Hundreds of odds and ends were plastered all over the T-shaped towers, covering them from top to bottom. Nine stood and stared at the bed-warming pans, colourful tea cosies, and griffin-shaped salt and pepper pots jutting out of the brickwork, along with dozens of items she couldn't even name, let alone imagine a use for.

As she looked at the shop, she wondered again where the Safekeeper was. She would find him, wherever he was hiding. There was a stab of guilt at not sharing her plan with Flabberghast, that she would be doing this in secret. But Nine felt herself harden. This was what she always did, wasn't it? She worked alone. She didn't – she couldn't – trust people with her secrets. Maybe her ma hadn't either...

"Make haste, Madam!" hissed Flabberghast, jumping in front of Nine's face and startling her. He grabbed her arm, opened the door and bundled everyone and the shopping basket inside.

CHAPTER 7

A little purple lizard perched on a shelf above the door and croaked an alert as they entered the shop. Flabberghast hurriedly closed the door behind them and peered anxiously out of the window. But Nine was more interested in what was *inside*.

Wobbly stacks of anything and everything were piled high everywhere – on the floor, on overloaded bending shelves, in large baskets that dangled from the ceiling.

It was like the Nest of a Thousand Treasures – the thieflings' den she had grown up in before she'd found the House – but magnified a million times. The old gang-master Pockets had loved collecting special treasures and knick-knacks. Old toby jugs, broken lockets, curious ornaments… She wondered what he would make of this shop.

Behind her, Eric was trying to shuffle her on but she could hardly move forwards, she was so surrounded by this … and that. At the very back of the shop she spotted a counter with a just-visible doorway behind it, covered with a curtain of vertical strips of material, all of which were sparkling and twinkling.

"No time for this," growled Spoon, stabbing his sword pointedly into an unsuspecting inflatable pumpkin beside the door. There was a small hiss of air from the pumpkin. "Where's Dish?"

Nine moved forwards, stepping over and ducking beneath a clatter of skeleton marionettes that dangled unnervingly from a chandelier. "This whole place looks like your cupboard under the stairs," she said to Flabberghast.

"Yes… Well… Purchases always seem like a good idea at the time."

Nine noticed a statue of a cat sitting on top of a pile of tea cosies, staring at her with sinister, pale green eyes. She leaned closer. "And what are *you* staring at?"

BANG. The purple lizard croaked again as the shop door flew open, bashing Flabberghast on the nose and knocking off his hat. But no one and nothing came through the doorway.

Suddenly there was that feeling again. The feeling of being watched.

Nine looked back at the cat statue and froze. The eyes were now looking in a different direction: just over Nine's shoulder...

She spun around. Still no one there.

"Welcome," said a wizard, slipping silently through the sparkling strips at the back of the shop and standing behind the polished, wooden counter. He had short dark hair streaked with grey and a short, pointy grey-black beard. He wore a bright red cloak with orange stripes that made Nine's eyes ache a little.

"Alfwin the Indubitably Dubitable at your service," he said, smiling widely and rubbing his hands together. His gaze lingered on Spoon for a moment, and the smallest of smiles crept across his face. Then his attention snapped back to Nine and the others. "What can I interest you in today? A bath for your frog?" He reached inside his cloak and pulled out a small lilypad-shaped dish. "Almost water-tight."

"No," said Flabberghast. He pulled his hat back on and stumbled towards them across the cluttered floor.

"Top quality weathervane. Fell off the back of a

house, if you know what I mean. Great condition. Works a treat, see?" He whisked out a weathervane in the shape of a dragon and blew and blew on it to make it spin. It didn't move an inch.

"No!" said Spoon, as Alfwin's puffed cheeks turned red with effort.

"That cat statue? From the mortal world. Can offer you a discount for today only."

"From my world? What's it doing here?" murmured Nine and looked again at the cat.

"Oh, you'd be surprised the things what pass from world to world," said Alfwin. "Tell you what: ten per cent off the cat. Just for you."

"No," said Nine.

"There must be something what takes your interest!" gasped a red-cheeked Alfwin, feebly holding up a little corked jar. "Repelling Song? Great for warding off green-horned minotaurs." His face fixed into a grimace as he uncorked the jar. A high-pitched, ear-splitting, wailing song burst out before Alfwin hastily slammed the cork back in.

"A huge improvement on *your* singing, lad," muttered Spoon.

Flabberghast cleared his throat, plonked a yonder on the counter and grabbed the jar. "May come in handy should they attack again," he muttered. Then he leaned forwards. "I don't suppose you might have anything that might give one's magic a little more … zap – if it happened to have … completely vanished?"

"I'm a dealer," said Alfwin, "not a miracle-worker."

Flabberghast sighed.

"There *is* something that takes our interest," said Nine, in a low but firm voice. "Your basement."

The wizard narrowed his eyes and threw the frog bath and the weathervane over his shoulder, where they shot through the curtain strips and landed with a slight crash. He looked shiftily left and right and twitched his moustache. He lowered his voice to barely a whisper. "The basement, eh? What's it worth?"

"Not getting stabbed," said Spoon, leaping up onto the wizard's shoulder and pointing his shiny new sword at Alfwin's throat.

But a glint in the wizard's eye made Nine's heart skip a beat. There was a crackle of crimson – and Spoon went flying off the wizard's shoulder and landed in a basket full of more little purple lizards that was dangling from the ceiling.

"How dare you!" roared Spoon, brushing a long scaly tail from the top of his head. One of the lizards licked his face, leaving a trail of saliva behind. Spoon swished his sword around again, first at the offending lizard and then in Alfwin's direction once more.

"Dr Spoon! Kindly refrain!" said Flabberghast, as Eric trundled over to the basket, raising his huge hand so that Spoon could clamber down onto him. Flabberghast turned to Alfwin the Indubitably Dubitable and smiled falsely. "Now, I am sure we could come to some arrangement…"

"I'm sure we can," said Alfwin, his eyes glinting again. "Always willing to trade a this for a that. What you got?" He nodded at Nine. "What you got in your satchel, mortal?"

"Nothing for you," Nine said, placing her arms protectively over the bag. A sense of panic filled her when she thought of her music box. But there was another flash of crimson – and a force sent the flap of her satchel flying open. Strands of magic twisted out from the fingertips of Alfwin's left hand and shot inside the bag, rooting around.

"Stop that!" Nine cried, but she was powerless against the magic. Anger crackled through her veins as she watched the crimson strands bring out the candle, her precious music box, the purse from Flabberghast, and the little velvet pouch she had pickpocketed from a witch at the Hopscotch Championship. The strands released the objects on the counter with a clatter then disappeared back into Alfwin's fingertips.

"Madam," said Flabberghast in a low voice, "I suggest you remain calm—"

"I AM CALM," Nine bellowed, glaring at Alfwin.

"Lady not," said Eric, beside her, wringing his tail.

"Just let him examine the objects, Madam—"

"BECAUSE I HAVE SO MUCH CHOICE ABOUT THAT—"

"—and we can come to an arrangement," finished Flabberghast. He smiled coldly at Alfwin, but Nine could see his nostrils flaring and his magic-less fingertips twitching. She could almost *feel* his frustration at being a powerless wizard. After three years of being under the curse, when he had been unable to use his magic – he had now lost it completely.

"Lass?" said Spoon in a low voice, clambering onto her shoulder.

"I'm fine," said Nine as she hardened her face into a scowl.

She watched Alfwin examine each object. She bit her lip as he held the candle close to his face, praying the flame didn't suddenly blow a raspberry, then breathed a sigh of relief as he simply sent it back to Nine's satchel with another crimson thread. Next he brought the music box closer to his face with a disappointed tut, before jiggling Flabberghast's purse, causing a jangling sound. "Just yonders," muttered Alfwin. "I need something a little bit special like."

Finally, he picked up the little pickpocketed velvet pouch and tipped the contents upside down onto the counter. Four coins, and a tiny, corked jar with sapphire-blue smoke swirling inside.

Alfwin's eyes lit up as he picked up the jar.

"Madam!" hissed Flabberghast, turning to Nine with wide eyes. "Wherever did you get that?"

Alfwin smirked. "A pretty sight and no mistake. Not often you come across a jar of Cloudsmoke."

"Cloudsmoke?" said Nine, staring at the jar.

"Allow me to demonstrate," Alfwin said smoothly. He carefully lifted the minuscule cork lid the merest fraction, revealing the smallest gap...

And a giant, whooshing cloud of sapphire smoke hurtled angrily out – billowing out into the shop and filling every corner. Nine was instantly swallowed up in thick, seething, airless blue, unable to see, panic rising. There was a rush of movement behind

77

her and sapphire smoke seemed to zoom past at an alarming rate, until her vision returned and she saw the vast cloud shrink as it was sucked back into the crack between the cork and the jar. The last wisp of smoke zoomed in and Alfwin pushed the cork down.

Silently and innocently, the smoke swirled lazily around inside the tiny bottle.

Alfwin looked like he was thinking hard, then he looked at Nine. "Come in handy, that, with the kind of folk I do business with." He nodded. "I'll take the jar, in return for a trip to the basement."

"You're welcome to it. Deal," said Nine.

"Deal," said Alfwin. At high speed, the crimson strands thrust the other items back into Nine's satchel and dropped the flap shut, then the magic retracted into his fingertips.

"Lady fine?" asked Eric, putting his rough hand on her shoulder.

"Lady always fine," said Nine. She glared at Alfwin the Indubitably Dubitable for good measure.

The wizard smiled a creeping smile. "Follow me, then." He beckoned to them and passed through the curtain of sparkling strips.

Nine, Flabberghast, Eric and Spoon exchanged uncertain glances.

"Right," muttered Nine. "Let's find ourselves a dish."

She led the others behind the counter, following the wizard through the curtain, trying hard to shake the feeling that someone – something – else was following *them*.

CHAPTER 8

They followed the shopkeeper down a narrow stone staircase. The deeper they went underground, the colder and damper it became and there was a smell of burning that seemed rather familiar.

Spoon hopped under Nine's shoulder and sniffed. "Too much ground amethyst," he muttered. "That will never work. Any moment now it'll go—"

BOOM. The small explosion forced a little puff of sickly-smelling lilac smoke up the staircase towards them. Nine spluttered, but Spoon smiled. It faded into nothing as they moved through the lilac smoke, but then they came to a sudden stop.

"We're here," Alfwin said, as Flabberghast almost walked into him.

"Oh dear," said Flabberghast.

Nine peered around him to see a closed wooden door with a small window in the middle. Emerald flames ran around the doorframe, as if they were sealing the door shut in a very you-will-never-open-this-again kind of way. Nine's heart sank.

"By any chance, has Ophidia the Unpredictable visited your shop of late?"

"Told you I'd take you to the basement." Alfwin shrugged. "Didn't say I'd be able to open the door."

There was the distant sound of a croaking purple lizard from the shop. "Customers," said Alfwin, rubbing his hands together. "I'll be back."

With a lot of oofing and squishing, Alfwin squeezed past everyone on the narrow staircase and headed back to the shop.

"Gahhh!" roared Spoon, leaping off Nine's shoulder, and landing on Flabberghast's hat. He stood on tiny tiptoes and peered in through the little window in the middle. "Professor Dish! She's in there!"

Nine, Flabberghast and Eric all suddenly pushed forward to look. Nine could just about see a dish with a wide-eyed face in the bottom of the bowl. She was working on a long wooden table, which was packed full of steaming glass beakers and bottles of all shapes and sizes filled with colourful liquids.

Dish narrowed her wide eyes as she cautiously lifted a phial over a bubbling pot, heated by a purple-flamed fire. She tipped the phial carefully, a drop trickled out…

"Dish!" Spoon cried as he banged on the window with his tiny fist.

The dish looked up. Her little mouth opened wide and she dropped the entire phial into the pot. There was a flash of lightning, and Dish ducked under the wooden bench as pink liquid whooshed out in a towering, sparkling fountain – before it all whooshed back into the pot again.

"Spoon! My goodness! What are you doing here?" she said, staring at them through the window.

"Finding you!" said Spoon.

"Oh, Spoon! It's good to see you! But we're in so much trouble! Have you had any success? I've not found the missing ingredient to make the…" Dish's voice trailed off and she looked at Spoon and the others uncertainly.

Nine saw Spoon flash Dish a quick warning look.

"Gold," Spoon said firmly.

"Gold," repeated Nine, narrowing her eyes.

"Gold," said Dish.

"Gold?" Nine folded her arms, looking accusingly at Spoon.

"Yes, Madam," said Flabberghast. He looked confused. "Dr Spoon has of course been attempting to discover the formula for gold. Somewhat unsuccessfully, I hasten to add. I've had to replace his bedroom door five times, his curtains twice, and you don't want to know what an explosion did to the chamber pot!"

Nine locked eyes with Spoon. His eyes burned into hers desperately. "Gold. Of course he has," said Nine.

"Spoon, I tried so hard to stay hidden while we searched for the missing ingredient. I don't know how Ophidia knew I was in Beyond, but she caught me and she's run out of patience. If I don't give the formula to her when she returns, I think it unlikely she'll spare my life!" Her little eyes brimmed with tears.

"Oooh!" said a voice from Nine's satchel. "Now *that's* trouble!" Flabberghast turned to Nine and frowned. Nine smiled quickly in return and tried to look as innocent as possible for someone stashing a forbidden, talking, unpaid-for candle in their satchel.

"Forgive me, Spoon. I should never have been tempted by a promise. Should never have agreed to create the … gold. But I swear I didn't know it was going to *her*!"

"Aye, and neither did I!"

"Neither did I," added Flabberghast, "should anyone be interested."

"It was Gazillion the Unstoppable who approached me," Dish continued, "and he said it was for someone incredibly dangerous. And that this person would grant me a powerful magical gift if I succeeded…" She gulped. "But be punished with unthinkable consequences if I failed. And, Spoon – I was so sure we could do it."

Spoon tugged at Flabberghast's hat. "We're only one flamin' step away from making gold. Let me get her safely back to my laboratory, then we will succeed or fail together."

"One thing I simply do not understand," Flabberghast said, turning to Spoon with a frown. "Why in the name of strawberry tea does my aunt want Dish to create gold? Surely she has wealth enough."

Dish and Spoon exchanged a shifty glance. "Well…" Dish began, but stopped abruptly as Alfwin shuffled his way down the cellar stairs.

Flabberghast narrowed his eyes at Dish but rotated round to face Alfwin, elbowing Nine in the ear as he did so. "You, Sir. We must release this dish and remove her from your basement."

Alfwin looked grim, but there was a definite glint in his eye. He pursed his lips and sucked in air noisily. "Oooh, don't know about that, now," he said, shaking his head. "I watched careful like when Ophidia cast that spell. Could break it easy enough but" – he raised his eyebrows – "it'd get me in a lot of trouble."

"Do it!" shouted Spoon.

"Don't know if you got anything worth me taking that risk…"

Spoon looked at Alfwin and growled through gritted teeth. "Name. Your. Price."

A creepy smile spread across Alfwin's face. "Fifty bars of your purest gold," he whispered, his eyes lighting up. "Before you leave Beyond. If you don't come with it here before closing time, I'll know." He leaned closer and smiled darkly. "I got eyes everywhere."

"Fine," said Spoon.

"Are you out of your wooden head?" Nine hissed.

"It's yours," continued Spoon, ignoring her. "Now set her free."

"Do we trust him?" Nine whispered to Flabberghast.

"Do we have a choice?" Flabberghast whispered back.

Nine sighed and strained her ears as Alfwin muttered something under his breath. Crimson strands shot from his fingertips again and entwined with the emerald flames running around the door. The flames fought back, trying to overpower the crimson strands, until they ran out of strength and fizzled out. The door opened into the basement room and Dish came running out, clutching a little suitcase.

Spoon leapt down from the wizard's shoulder towards Dish, and she threw a spindly arm around his shoulders.

"To the House," said Spoon. "We don't have much time." He cast a look at Flabberghast, then Dish and Spoon hopped over everyone and ran up the stone steps towards the shop floor.

Eric, Flabberghast and Nine unsquished themselves enough to walk up the steps after them. Nine looked over her shoulder as they went. Alfwin the Indubitably Dubitable leaned against the doorframe, arms folded, smiling smugly.

"See you later," he said in a low, threatening voice.

Nine gave him a withering look that could topple a tower and headed up to the shop.

Dish and Spoon were already at the front door, whispering. Nine saw them jump a little when she, Eric and Flabberghast came through the sparkly curtain strips at the doorway to the shop. And as they entered, Nine immediately had that feeling again: there was someone else... Something else...

She passed the cat statue, leaned towards it and narrowed her eyes. The cat was still looking over Nine's shoulder.

"You can see it, can't you?" Nine whispered to the statue. "Someone's following me, aren't they?" A little shiver ran down Nine's spine as the cat's eyes shifted to look directly at Nine, and a little smile spread over its face. But it remained completely silent.

Nine huffed. "Keep your secrets, then."

The purple lizard croaked again as Flabberghast opened the door. They all stepped out into the street, followed by their basket. And Nine's heart skipped a beat. Because there, in the middle of the alleyway opposite them, with a shopping basket just behind him, was Gazillion the Unstoppable.

CHAPTER 9

Nine stared at Flabberghast, who was rooted to the spot. The floating shopping basket floated into him, nudging him a step forward.

"Aha!" Gazillion declared triumphantly. He flicked back his green-tinged hair. "We meet once more, Flabberghast the Unworthy! Revenge will be—" Gazillion glanced down to Dish and his eyes widened in disbelief and rage. "What are YOU doing out here?!"

Nine stared back defiantly. "Running!" she yelled, shoving Flabberghast forward and grabbing Eric's hand from behind. Flabberghast ran, his star-speckled cloak flapping behind him. Nine followed, dragging the troll, as Spoon and the suitcase-clutching Dish held hands and skittered and scuttled in and out of their legs. The shopping basket zoomed along behind them all contentedly.

Nine glanced back to see Gazillion rising up in the air, his cloak puffing out like terrible mauve wings.

"You know, I liked him much better when he was a turnip. To the House!" called Flabberghast, as they darted down an alleyway between a shop shaped like a bottle of ink with a feathered quill sticking out of the roof, and another shaped like a huge purple goblet with stars dotted all over it.

They darted on, dodging the overhanging balconies and turreted towers of the houses. But Gazillion was still hot on their heels. "Bring back that dish!" he cried, the air billowing his cloak as he flew.

Nine heard some soft crashing sounds and looked over her shoulder to see his shopping basket hurtling desperately after him, walloping him on the back, the shoulder and even knocking the wizard's hat off as it tried to keep pace. The wizard turned and glowered at it as he plonked his hat back on his head.

"OOF! You intolerable basket! Mind your step or I, Gazillion the Unstoppable, will turn you into a plant pot!" He turned his attention back to them. "Come back immediately! You *dare* to defy Ophidia the Unpredictable!"

"Yes, we flippin' do!" Nine yelled over her shoulder, then turned to look ahead. Her heart thumped as she caught sight of the House. She'd never felt so happy to see the dishevelled building.

Flabberghast hurled himself at the front door. As though it knew they were coming, it flew open immediately and he, Nine, Eric, Dish, Spoon – and the shopping basket – tumbled inside. Flabberghast slammed the door shut and everyone threw their backs against it. The shopping basket collapsed to the floor, spilling its contents across the hall.

There was a pummelling on the door.

"Ha! Doors will not protect you, Flabberghast the Unworthy!" came Gazillion's voice. "Ophidia the Unpredictable wants that formula. And I, Gazillion the Unstoppable, shall have the greatest delight informing her that you have broken her spell and removed that impudent piece of crockery. That dish had better have the formula ready when she comes for you, or else!"

"Or else what?" Nine growled back.

There was the clearing of a throat and the embarrassed shuffling of feet outside the door. "Well... I don't know, do I?" grumbled Gazillion awkwardly. "She's unpredictable. That's the whole point." His voice grew in confidence. "BUT! It will not be a pleasant experience for you, only for me. For I will be watching, and, Flabberghast the Unworthy, I shall be laughing! Until our next meeting, then!" The sound of footsteps faded into the distance.

Nine allowed herself a brief sigh of relief, then moved over to the letterbox cupboard fixed to the wall on the right-hand side of the door. She opened the little cupboard and poked her hand through the letterbox flap to prop it open – and peeped outside. Gazillion was strutting back through the House Park, flicking back his green-blond hair and wagging a finger at the shopping basket which now seemed to be deliberately and rather sulkily butting into him at every available opportunity.

"So nice having him around," she said, letting the letterbox snap shut.

Flabberghast sighed. He surveyed the contents of the shopping basket on the plum hallway carpet, then put the empty basket outside the front door, where it dropped contentedly to the ground, flopping its handles down gratefully by its sides.

"Ah, not quite yet," said Flabberghast. "Go and find the skeleton and the gargoyle."

The basket flapped its handles irritably for a moment, and then sped off through the House Park.

Spoon turned to Dish. "He only mentions you," he said thoughtfully. "They still don't know I hold half the formula?"

"Oh no," said Dish. "I kept that secret safe."

Nine watched as a strange blush appeared at the sides of Dish's face. Dish held Spoon's gaze for a moment and then looked down at her tiny feet.

Spoon twitched his moustache from side to side. "I knew I could trust you. I would have done the same for you, lass," he said, grabbing Dish's little hand. His voice softened. "We are in this together. Come to my laboratory. We'll try again to make this gold, lass, if it's the last thing we do."

"It may well be the last thing you do, judging by your cremated curtains at the last attempt, Dr Spoon," said Flabberghast.

Spoon ignored him and began to guide Dish to the staircase, but Nine swiftly moved in front of them, blocking the stairs.

"I still have some questions. You need to sort the formula for what, exactly?" she said. "And *don't* tell me it's gold."

Spoon stared at her. Then he glanced at Dish. "Granted, it's ... not *exactly* gold, lass. But I would nae ask too many questions if I were you."

"Spoon, tell us what's going on!" said Nine.

"All I will tell you is that Dish made a deal and I agreed to help her in this dangerous quest. It turns out we owe your blasted aunt this formula; so we give her this formula." Spoon glanced at Flabberghast. "Then, with a bit of luck, lad, she will leave us all in peace." He skittered off to the main staircase, pulling Dish behind.

"Or pieces," said Flabberghast gloomily.

"Aunt scary," said Eric.

"She's the worst aunt in all the realms. Apart from possibly her younger sister, Aunt Griselda the Unruly." Flabberghast grimaced. "In my experience, younger sisters are troublesome at best, deadly at worst. Life is certainly more pleasant without mine." He sighed. "If it wasn't for her, I'd still have my magic. Flabberghast the Unworthy … by name and nature."

"Flabby tea," said Eric, patting the wizard's arm before lolloping off towards the tea cupboard.

Nine turned to Flabberghast. "Listen. Whatever this not-exactly-gold is, I don't like the idea of it in the hands of Ophidia. Could we not outrun her? If we did the rest of our shopping quickly and—"

"Tea cupboard!" rumbled Eric.

ZAP. Nine became a skeleton wearing a satchel. Eric was rapidly turning every shade of the rainbow.

And Flabberghast transformed into his sister. Nine stared in disbelief as the pretend-witch smiled at Nine and wiggled her fingers in a wave. Then she tossed her scarlet hair before morphing back into Flabberghast, who shuddered.

"Brrr! I can see why Bonehead wanted socks," said Nine, rubbing her re-fleshed arms to warm up.

"No, Madam, we cannot outrun my aunt," said Flabberghast. "And even if we could, how long for? She would hunt us down! *And* she is merciless! There's never been a happy ending for any witch or wizard who has stood in her way. You should have seen what she did to my Uncle Mortimer the Unwise. We have no option but to give her what she seeks."

"And what is it exactly that she seeks? Why does she want gold that is not-exactly-gold?"

"I have no idea, Madam!"

Nine felt a million questions whirring through her brain. "And even if Dish and Spoon get the formula right, Alfwin the Indubitably Dubitable is expecting actual gold. So, what will we tell him when we hand over not-exactly-gold?"

"I do not know, Madam!"

"And why—?"

"MADAM!" said Flabberghast, grabbing fistfuls of his curly auburn hair. "Truly, you are a question mark poorly disguised as a mortal!"

"You have no idea of all the questions I have!" Nine shot back.

Flabberghast frowned at her, thoughtfully. Eric plonked down a teapot and some teacups onto the kitchen table. He eyed Nine, looking sad and uncertain.

"Lady questions," he said. "Eric help?"

RECEIVED WITH THANKS, THE SAFEKEEPER.

Nine felt the same stab of guilt as she thought of the note. But this was *her* ma, *her* secret. And she didn't know what to think or who to trust. Her ma? Flabberghast? Eric?

"No," Nine said decisively, as much to herself as anyone else. "Sorry. Eric can't help."

The troll's tail drooped a little.

Nine softened her voice. "I just ... need some space."

Flabberghast propelled Nine down the hallway towards the front door.

"Then the best solution, Madam, for all of us, is that you take a nice breath of fresh air."

As they reached the front door and stepped over the pile of shopping, a soft explosion came from upstairs, knocking the portrait of Ethel the Continually Hopping (1719–1798) off the wall. Nine and Flabberghast sighed in unison.

"Go to the Secret Shop of Secrets. The message urn rumours say there's a new owner. One can only hope they are more efficient than Dracona the Infuriatingly Blabber-mouthed."

"Why? What did Dracona—?"

Flabberghast opened the front door. "Just go and buy a secret."

"But how on earth can you buy—?"

"No more questions!" wailed Flabberghast. "I'm beginning to understand how the Asking Stone felt." He shoved Nine outside and slammed the door.

Nine went to the letterbox mounted to the left of the front door. She prised open the flap and yelled through the slot, "Just one more: where is the shop?"

There was just the gargled, voice-breaking wail of an exasperated wizard in reply.

"Fine, I'll find it myself," Nine snapped into the letterbox. She turned to head towards the town.

"Ooooh, you're in trouble!" giggled a voice in her satchel.

"Ssshhh," said Nine, giving the satchel a rough pat

as she headed through the House Park. "Remember they don't know about you, and you don't exist."

She stepped back out onto the cobbled street, still bustling with witches and wizards of all ages. A witch floated in the air, carrying a tray around her neck bearing steaming goblets. Judging by the smell, Nine guessed the ingredients consisted largely of puréed slugs and dragon manure and walked on by.

There were dozens of shops in all shapes and sizes. She walked past a seven-storey hopscotch sports shop, in the shape of a giant, towering golden hopscotch grid, with each golden number etched onto a window. Next to it was a shop in the shape of an open umbrella standing upright on its handle. The whole building twirled around slowly on the spot, with witches and wizards queuing to jump in through the door in the handle when it next came around.

Then there was a plant shop in the shape of a flowerpot, which sprouted brightly coloured flowers and puffed out a sweet, tempting perfume as she went by. But despite all the many wonderful and curious buildings, there was no sign of a secrets shop.

As she passed the house maintenance shop in the shape of a feather duster, she saw Bonehead skipping along, dangling an open parasol over his shoulder and carrying what looked like a cage under a black cloth – suspiciously like the padlocked one she had seen through the snake-eye window. Cas still wore the huge, flowery hat and scurried beside him carrying what appeared to be a lamp in the shape of a star. The shopping basket had obviously caught up with them, and had now been filled with various weird and wonderful items.

"Oi!" Nine called and ran over to the skeleton and the gargoyle.

"I've bought a toothbrush!" boomed Bonehead, barely containing his delight. "A toothbrush! I haven't brushed my teeth in years."

"Well," said Nine, "to be fair, you haven't eaten in years, either. Er, Bonehead, that cage—"

"And now I am going to buy some cushions for my closet! Help the old joints." He looked at Nine and paused for a moment with what was possibly meant to be a grin, but his expression didn't change at all. Then the skeleton strode onwards.

Nine bit her lip. The cage really did look like the padlocked one.

"That cage—" she called after him, but Cas edged closer to her.

"Reckon I found who you was lookin' for," the gargoyle said, looking very pleased with herself.

Nine's heart gave a little leap as her thoughts turned from the cage to the torn parchment. "Where, Cas? Where is the Safekeeper?"

"Ssshhh!" said Cas, putting a stony finger to her lips. "Stone the crows! Fine gargoyle you'd make. Don'tcha know nothin' about keepin' secrets?"

The words cut Nine and there was the familiar stab of guilt. Maybe she was better at keeping secrets than anyone knew. "Where is the you-know-who?"

"Well," said Cas, "rumour has it that today he's doin' his business where people do their business, if you get what I mean."

Nine stared at the gargoyle blankly. "What?"

"Their *business*," repeated Cas, winking.

Nine just frowned.

The gargoyle sighed. "He's around the back of the Chamber Pot. Blimey. I ain't never payin' you to do no spyin'."

"Thank you! And, Cas?" Inside Nine, the guilt swarmed and stung. "Don't say anything to anyone, especially to Flabberghast. Just our secret."

The gargoyle rolled her stony eyes. "That's if you don' yell it from the blimmin' rooftops!" She scurried after Bonehead.

"Oooh! Now what are we going to do?" the candle in her satchel piped up.

"The Secret Shop can wait," Nine murmured. "I've got a secret of my own to sort out first."

CHAPTER 10

As Nine approached the chamber pot-shaped building with desperate witches and wizards hurtling towards it, she had to admit it was a good place to do business. It was not the kind of place people wanted to hang around. And the people who did come here had more important things on their minds than poking around to see if there was anything unusual going on.

Except Nine.

She tried to stroll casually past the line of wizards and witches, many of whom were standing with their legs crossed. At the back of the building, Nine cast her eyes around. There didn't seem to be anything odd or unusual. She mooched past the

101

poster of the wanted toilet. It briefly crossed her mind to enquire about the reward, before deciding that Flabberghast would probably never forgive her for handing over their only proper toilet. There was a pile of discarded, chipped and broken flowery chamber pots with ominous-looking stains inside, heaped up on the dusty ground against the curved wall of the building. She didn't fancy investigating those. No one with a grain of sense would want to investigate those...

Unless...

That was the whole point.

Nine wrinkled her nose and stepped closer to the pile.

"Oooh, I don't think this is going to end well!" said the candle, its little flame now poking out from the satchel.

Nine looked around her. Nothing. No one. She reached towards the handle of a purple chamber pot with white flowers on the top of the pile.

"Something's gonna go wrong!" sang the candle.

"Shut up!" hissed Nine. "I'm only going to move these chamber pots and see if they're hiding anything underneath."

Was this a good idea?

She reached out and grasped the handle of the purple chamber pot. Suddenly, an eye appeared in the base. Nine gasped and released the handle.

The eye stared at Nine.

Nine stared back.

"Er ... hello," she whispered. "I want to see the Safekeeper."

There was a silvery flash from the eye which dazzled Nine. Everything in her vision turned to bright silver and she had a sickening feeling of falling. The silvery-ness faded away and Nine rubbed her aching eyes as her vision returned.

"I said something was gonna go wrong," whispered the candle in the satchel.

And, as Nine saw silvery ropes begin to twist around her ankles like living snakes, she had to agree.

Nine stood in a cold, dark cellar lit by candles, rooted to the spot by the rope-snakes, which now reached up to her knees. A network of pipes ran above her, and down the sides of the damp, gloomy room. It smelled of something forgotten, mixed with an odour of something rather unpleasant.

A wrinkly wizard in a maroon cloak sat behind an empty wooden table. Around each table leg wound more silvery rope-snakes, looking ready to strike if needed. The wizard rested his elbows on top of the table and peered at Nine. His hair was grey, frizzy and seemed to grow sideways out of his head. His skin was deathly pale, as though he hadn't seen the light of day for several years. He stared at Nine with eyes that twinkled with mischief from behind small, round spectacles.

The only noise was the sound of slow, persistent dripping from the ceiling, and surely the sound of Nine's heart, which seemed to fill the cellar. There was no door. No window. No way out.

Nine tried to move her legs but the ropes made an ominous hissing noise and tightened even more.

"Not exactly a warm welcome to your customers," Nine said, telling herself she was only shaking because of the cold, which reached right into her bones.

"Storing or collecting?" the wizard said in a low, gravelly voice.

"What – what do you mean?" Nine asked.

"Two reasons people come to the Safekeeper," the wizard rumbled on gruffly. "Storing an object. Or collecting an object."

"Collecting," she said, trying to sound bolder than she felt. "Something that belonged to my ma."

"And what would that be?" the Safekeeper asked cautiously.

"I – I don't know. I just know she left it with you before she died."

The Safekeeper lowered his head and peered over his spectacles. "That's tricky, isn't it, then? It's not yours."

"But my ma would want me to have it!"

"Would she now? Lots of reasons people leave an object with the Safekeeper. You don't even know what the item is."

The words chilled Nine. What had her ma been up to? Why had she done a secret deal with this strange wizard in this strange cellar? What if this something was dangerous and Nine wasn't meant to have it?

"But I tell you something, Missy." The wizard leaned closer. "If something's left with the Safekeeper, there's usually more than one person wants it." He broke into a smile and his eyes gleamed again.

Nine bit her lip. It hurt that she knew so little about her ma. What *was* it that Flabberghast had refused to tell her? Thoughts rolled around in her head as the Safekeeper smirked at her. What should she do now? Should she try to find it? Leave the secret buried as her ma had left it?

"Not so sure now, Missy?" He clasped his hands together, lifted them up towards his face and rested his chin on his fingers. "Do you want it? Or do you not?"

Nine hesitated. If only she knew more about anything. She felt like she was standing on the edge of a cliff, not knowing if she was going to fly or fall...

"You're wasting my time," said the Safekeeper. "I don't like time-wasters."

He clicked his wrinkled fingers. The silver rope-snakes began to twist higher, and higher... Around her waist... Nine fought back the panic.

The ropes twisted higher... Across her chest...

Can't breathe!

Reaching for her throat...

"I want it!" she cried. She breathed quickly, trying to calm herself down. The shimmering rope-snakes hissed disappointedly and slid back down to her ankles. "Where is it?"

The Safekeeper smiled. "Safe," he said. "And you can only open it with a key. No key, no deal."

Nine clenched her fists. "I haven't got a key!" she said. Fear began to give way to frustration.

"You sure about that?" The Safekeeper looked over his spectacles at Nine again. "Your ma didn't leave you one?"

"No, Ma didn't leave me anything!"

Except...

Nine's hand shot inside the satchel.

"Ooh, that tickles!" whispered the candle.

Nine pulled out her music box and stared at it. The only thing her ma had left her...

The Safekeeper smiled. "Now we're talking. I remember this one. Years ago." He eyed the music box. "A key that looks like a key – too obvious. Anyone can see that. But a key that looks like anything ... could be anything. It's there. Right under your nose. And you don't even know it."

Nine stared at the Safekeeper then looked again at the music box in her slightly shaking hand. This was the key? The key to something her ma had wanted to keep safe. But...

"How?" said Nine. "How does it unlock something?"

"Play the music," said the Safekeeper.

With trembling fingers, Nine turned the handle on the music box. She thought of all the times the music box had played in Pockets' Nest, the den of thieves where she had lived. The music had comforted her then. But now, as the gentle, tinkling music echoed through the dank, shadowy cellar, it made Nine feel unnerved. All this time, *right under your nose...*

"No," said the Safekeeper.

Nine stopped instantly and the music box silenced. She eyed the wizard suspiciously as his eyes gleamed.

"Not that way. Everyone plays it that way, don't they? Too easy."

Nine stared at the music box. "Not that way? There's only one way to play a music box!"

A half-smile crept across the Safekeeper's face. He looked very pleased with himself. "Is there?"

Nine rolled the handle thoughtfully between her cold fingers. Surely you could only turn the handle forwards to play the music box. Unless...

She gripped the handle tighter, and – holding her breath – she turned it slowly backwards towards her. To her amazement, there was a chaotic twinkle of incomprehensible notes and then—

WHOOMPF! Nine jumped and nearly dropped the music box. A little rolled-up scroll popped out of nowhere in front of the Safekeeper's face. The scroll unrolled and the wizard began to read something.

"Well, well," said the Safekeeper. "We have an unlocking."

"What?" said Nine. "What does it say?"

There was a little *pffffft* and the scroll disappeared in a puff of yellow smoke.

"The location where she chose to have the item hidden. Don't keep all the valuable objects here in one place, do I? That don't sound safe to me. Anyone could break in and steal them."

Nine felt frustration rising in her. Why couldn't anything be even remotely easy? "So where is it? Where is the thing my ma left?"

The flickering of candlelight danced on the Safekeeper's face. "Whatever it is she left, you'll find it at the Bookshop at the Back of Beyond. You can clear off now."

"But ... how do I know what I'm looking for when I get there?"

"Not my problem," said the Safekeeper. "Have to hope your ma thought of that."

"But what if I—?"

The Safekeeper rolled his eyes. "Anyone ever said you ask too many questions?"

"Well, maybe," said Nine crossly, "but how can I—?"

The Safekeeper waved his hand. There was the feeling of rope-snakes releasing her ankles from their grip, then a silvery glare filled Nine's vision once more.

When it passed, she found herself standing beside the pile of chamber pots, still clutching her music box. Her mind reeled.

"Well, now you've gone and done it, haven't you? I said you'd go and do it and you have," chattered the voice inside her satchel.

Nine stared at the music box in disbelief. All this time – *all this time* – she had kept the music box, completely unaware that it held the key to … something. Something important. She tucked the precious box back into the satchel and fished out the candle. The little flame with the candle's face popped out of the wick.

"You'd better tell your friends about this!"

"No," said Nine. "And remember – you don't exist. So, you're not allowed to tell anyone anything about this either. No blabbing."

"Blab? Ooh, I don't blab! Just, you know, like to have a bit of a chinwag now and again – well, pretty much all the time."

"Well, don't," Nine said sharply.

"It's just I really think you ought to tell your

friends because this seems reeeeally dodgy and reeeeally dangerous and—"

"NO," Nine snapped. "I'll do this by myself."

"Suit yourself."

"I will," said Nine. "I always will."

"And that's your problem!" the candle said.

"When I want your opinion, I'll ask for it. You may be waiting a while!" Nine said, regretting her harsh words as soon as they left her mouth.

The candle blew another large raspberry at Nine and extinguished itself. Nine huffed and put the candle back into her satchel.

"Not helping you find the bookshop now," muttered the candle sulkily from inside the bag.

"I don't need your help anyway."

But as Nine walked through the town, those words felt uneasy. Until she had found the House at the Edge of Magic, she had spent her life alone. Dealing with her problems and her secrets alone. She thought of the troll's drooping tail. And of the candle's pleading.

Doubt crept like a nervous, twitching shadow. But she had no time for it.

She had a bookshop to find.

CHAPTER 11

It wasn't difficult to work out what the bookshop was going to look like – but Nine still had to find it in the maze of Beyond. She walked and walked through the cobbled streets, occasionally rolling her ankles on the uneven stones. She felt like she had been magically shrunk to the size of a beetle, weaving amongst oversized, everyday items.

She walked on further until she passed the anvil-shaped blacksmith's shop, and a huge purple teapot decorated with strawberries. It smelled wonderful, but this was no time for tea.

After the teapot, the shops ran out, replaced by occasional ramshackle stalls of witches and wizards selling dodgy-looking charms, or goods. The streets were almost empty of customers. Surely she had reached the back of Beyond!

And then, there it was, all by itself at the end of a bumpy stone path. It had a huge, purple roof shaped like an open book perched on top of the building, which was dotted with windows. A large bay window jutted out on the right, and on the left, a curving set of steps made of books led to the front door.

Nine stared in amazement. All those floors. All those books. It was like a dream. But even more importantly, she longed to find out what it was that her ma had safely stowed away somewhere within its walls. She needed to find it, and she needed to find it quickly. Dish and Spoon were probably putting the finishing touches to their formula and then they had to get away from Ophidia as soon as possible.

Nine ran enthusiastically up the book-steps. But as she reached the front door, her heart sank. There was a blind pulled down over the door and a rusty, creaking sign hanging near by said "Open in 5". Nine folded her arms and tutted. Then she watched in amazement as the words seemed to erase themselves and new writing appeared: "Open after lunch." Followed by a hastily scrawled addition underneath: "Probably." And then another: "Possibly."

Nine sighed and went around to the bay window on the right. She cupped her hands around her eyes to peer through the grimy window. There were bookshelves galore! Books beyond books were stacked everywhere, higgledy-piggledy in piles that nearly touched the ceiling, stuffed on shelves, even lining the staircases that went up and down to the different floors. It looked incredible. She longed to be inside, to search the books, to smell them… What incredible books could be lurking inside a magical bookshop?

"It's shut," Nine muttered, half hoping the candle could hear her.

"Are you talking to me?" the candle said sulkily. "Does that mean we're friends again? I'm not sure if I want to be friends again."

"We can be friends," Nine said stiffly. "Just maybe talk a little bit less."

"Then maybe be grumpy a little bit less," said the candle.

"Fine, it's a deal," said Nine awkwardly. "The bookshop's shut."

"Ohhh dear," said the candle. "You know, it's not been the same since the bookseller left all those years ago."

The bookseller. They would have known all those magical books inside out and known exactly what to recommend. Just like Mr Downes used to do for Nine at the library. She felt a pang as she thought of the dear librarian. He would probably have loved to get his hands on all these books.

"It's ever so tricky-some, that shop now. But ooh, it's a bookshop, isn't it, so it's still going to be ever so brilliant."

Nine felt herself warm a little towards the candle again. She wondered how many books it had read, lighting the pages for readers late into the night.

Nine was desperate to go inside. She ran around the other side of the shop, peering through more windows. Somewhere in there was the item her ma had been hiding...

"Wretched shop! Cease this infuriating closure! Will you never open?" roared a turnippy, wizardy voice from the front of the shop.

Nine pushed herself flat against the wall of the bookshop and held her breath. There was the sound of increasingly frustrated knocking. "Ophidia the Unpredictable must complete her shopping and *you* are preventing her. I, Gazillion the Unstoppable, demand you open up!" There was the sound of kicking at the door. "Do not blame me if she reduces you to ashes! And I am not called Gazillion the Unstoppable for nothing! I will not be deterred by a mere door!"

Nine listened to the wizard's repeated knocking and kicking and ranting.

"Yes, well," said Gazillion, puffing and panting after a short while. "Just to be clear, door: I am still unstoppable." He lowered his voice and spoke quickly. "I'm just, you know, having a quick comfort break."

At the sound of hastily departing footsteps, Nine poked her head around the corner of the building, to see Gazillion walking in a very funny, very fast waddle – she guessed in the direction of the giant chamber pot. "The sooner we get away from Gazillion and Ophidia, the better," she muttered to the candle. She didn't like being stuck in the same place as them one little bit.

"Better crack on with your shopping, then," said a voice from the satchel.

The Secret Shop...

"Where is the Secret Shop?"

"You're lucky I happen to know this place like the back of my flame. Ooh, been all over I have, just I keep getting taken back to the candle shop and—"

116

Nine lifted the flap of her satchel and peered inside, huffing at the little scorch marks dotted everywhere. "Can't think why. Fine. So where is the Secret Shop?"

"It's a secret," giggled the candle.

Nine gave the satchel a little shake. "If you don't start being a bit more helpful, *I* am going to take you back to the candle shop, as well!"

"Oh, all right, grumpy," said the candle good-naturedly. "Take five steps to your left."

"What?"

"Go on, take five steps to your left."

Nine sighed and took five sidesteps.

"Now go five steps to your right."

Nine sighed again and took five sidesteps to her right. "I'm back where I started!" The candle giggled. "Just checking you were listening."

Nine shook the satchel again.

"All right, all right," giggled the candle. "Walk down the other side of the bookshop until you reach the back."

Nine walked past the bookshop, then suddenly, there was that feeling again. Of someone – something – behind her. The hairs on the back of her neck prickled. Her palms became slightly sweaty...

She turned around suddenly.

She scanned the area with the sharp eyes of a thief. Nothing. No one.

There was a sudden, silent rush of something flying past her – ahead of her – which made the hairs on the back of her neck stand up. She looked frantically around but there was still nothing to be seen.

"Here we are," chirped the candle, breaking her thoughts.

Nine stared. There was nothing in front of her, not even a cobbled path. It was probably the kind of thing that only people who knew what they were looking for … knew what they were looking for. And Nine had no idea.

"I'd put your hands out, if I were you," said the candle.

Nine put her hands in front of her, walking slowly, carefully. If there was one thing the world of magic had taught her it was not to believe her own eyes.

And she was right. Her outstretched hands bumped into the warm smooth feeling of wood. Invisible, secret wood. She felt all around it.

"A door," breathed Nine.

"Open it," whispered the candle. "Go on. Dare you." There was a little giggle.

Nine's hands tracked over the invisible wood until she touched something cool and metal. Her heart thumping, Nine twisted the handle and the door opened inwards. The room beyond was dimly lit and Nine could see nothing beyond the brown doormat that lay just inside. The word "SHHH" was spelled out in blood-red letters across the mat.

Holding her breath, Nine stepped inside.

And the door clicked quietly shut behind her.

CHAPTER 12

Nine stood on the doormat, frozen to the spot, plunged into darkness. The same sparkling, red letters from the doormat appeared in front of her in the air, this time spelling the words:

YOU HAVE A SECRET.

Then they faded away to nothing.

"No, I haven't," Nine whispered, but her voice was defiant. One thing she'd learned from her days as a pickpocket: deny everything.

YOU LIE, spelled out the blood-red letters. In a flash, they transformed into sparkling ribbons and hurtled at Nine's satchel, grabbing and snatching at the flap. One or two wormed their way inside.

"Oooh!" squeaked the candle inside the satchel. "That tickles!"

"Fine, all right! All right!" said Nine, flapping her hand at the scarlet ribbons. They slowly and calmly retracted and reshaped to form letters.

YOU WANT TO BUY A SECRET.

"Yes, I have to," Nine said uneasily.

TELL ME ALL ABOUT IT, coaxed the letters.

"No," said Nine, as they faded away. She folded her arms. "I don't even know who I'm talking to. Who are you? What are you?"

IT'S A SECRET, spelled the letters. Then they jiggled up and down a little, as if they were silently laughing, before fading into the darkness.

Nine sighed impatiently. "Well, can I actually see what I'm supposed to be looking at in here? Or is that a secret, too?"

There was silence and stillness for a moment. Then the red ribbons appeared and moved over to the far left of Nine. They flew upwards towards the ceiling – if there was one – and, as they did, they lit up shelf after shelf packed with clear bottles and jars. Each vessel had a different coloured jumble of letters, which seemed to be swirling around slowly inside. Nine stared as the ribbons twisted and climbed

121

higher and higher, revealing still more shelves and bottles, before fading away into the distance. There must have been *hundreds* of shelves.

"Are they all secrets?" Nine whispered.

The blood-red letters appeared and floated around Nine in a circle. She read them before they faded.

YES. BUY ONE. GO ON.

"Fine," said Nine. "Then I can leave." She reached inside her satchel and pulled out the little purse of coins that Flabberghast had given her. "How many yonders?"

The sparkling letters appeared in front of her, word by word, before disappearing:

YOU DO NOT PAY WITH COIN.

"Then what exactly do I pay with?" A little prickling of unease ran up her spine and into her brain.

TO BUY A SECRET

YOU SELL A SECRET.

Nine stared, watching the last sparkle of letters disappear. Why had Flabberghast sent her here? Something wasn't right. She didn't even know who she was dealing with. But what choice did she have? They needed something from this shop, or the House couldn't leave.

"Fine. I can tell you what I have in my satchel," she offered, slyly.

NO.

The letters faded and then reappeared – bolder this time.

YOUR DEEPEST, DARKEST SECRET.

Frustration bubbled up inside Nine like an extremely fed-up volcano. She put her hands on her hips. "I don't have a big secret!"

EVERYONE HAS SECRETS, DO THEY NOT?

"Fine," said Nine. She was running out of options. "I do have a deep, dark secret. My secret is … I have been to see the Safekeeper."

As she spoke, her words appeared all around her in blue, sparkling letters. They were beautiful, terrible, and Nine was relieved as they too faded away to nothing.

SOMEONE SHARES THAT SECRET. YOU MUST OFFER A SECRET NEVER TOLD TO A SOUL.

Never told to a soul? Well... There *was* something no one else knew...

THAT FILLS YOU WITH SUCH SHAME.

Yes, something she held and stored in her heart, that had weighed it down with guilt ever since that day. Something she hated to think about. Nine felt all squirmy inside.

GO ON, coaxed the letters. DO TELL.

"Once," began Nine, in a voice that wavered slightly, "I pickpocketed Mr Downes. A librarian … and a good man."

MORE.

"And … I stole a locket." She shuffled awkwardly at the memory. How could she have done this to the dear librarian? The one who had saved her so many times, and in so many ways. But desperation could drive someone to unbelievable depths.

A LOCKET?

"Yes, with strange markings around the edge on the back and some words, I think. I can't really remember. I've taken many things. I know it was broken – it would never open – but I took it back to Pockets for his nest. He liked it anyway." She opened her eyes and stared down at her feet. "He gave me some bread as a reward. The locket's hung from a beam in the ceiling ever since."

The words Nine had spoken appeared again in blue, sparkling letters. She stared at them in horror and loathing as they swirled around. Some words seemed to burn into Nine's eyes more than others: MR DOWNES LIBRARIAN GOOD MAN STOLE LOCKET TOOK POCKETS.

Then, out of nowhere, a large, corked glass jar appeared in the air beside them. The cork popped out and the sparkly words hurtled in, pushing and shoving and jiggling around. As the last letter darted inside the jar, the cork wedged itself in place. The jar floated up and up towards one of the shelves. Nine watched it until the last trace of blue letters was lost in the blackness.

WHAT A TERRIBLY NAUGHTY THING TO DO.

Nine felt sudden, angry tears burning behind her eyes. She leaned forwards into the darkness. "You have no idea what it was like!"

OH, BUT I DO.

Nine felt her anger waver, replaced by uncertainty. "No, you don't." She glanced up at the jar again. "You know nothing about my life!" she insisted.

OH

BUT

I

DO.

The letters jiggled again as if they were laughing.

"You're lying!" shouted Nine. "How could you possibly know?"

IT'S A SECRET.

Nine gazed at the shelves. All those secrets… If people told secrets about other people…

125

The blood-red letters jiggled again.

YOU HAVE SOLD A SECRET. NOW YOU MAY BUY ONE.

Suddenly the scarlet ribbons flew towards Nine. She instinctively put her hands up to her head, but the ribbons wound themselves around her waist instead. She yelped as they pulled her upwards in the air, through airless darkness, past hundreds of higgledy-piggledy shelves of glowing bottles and jars.

"Stop!" cried Nine, as she tried to catch her breath. "Slow down!"

Nine shrieked as one of the blood-red ribbons unwrapped itself from Nine's waist, making her drop a little in the air, before one of the other ribbons leapt up to catch her. The unwrapped ribbon spelled the words:

CHOOSE YOUR SECRET.

"How should I know which one to choose?"

TRUST YOUR INSTINCTS. LIKE A THIEF.

"I don't pick pockets any more," Nine shot back.

The sparkling ribbon changed itself into a tiny skull, a bottle with something swirling inside, and two coins, which rotated on their end. The contents of the stolen purse.

Nine gasped. How could the letters know? How could they possibly know she had pickpocketed a

126

witch when she went to the Hopscotch Championship?

MORE SECRETS?

Had someone seen her take it? Sold it as a secret in exchange for another? Panic began to flood through her.

TRUST, THIEF.

Trust her instincts? What was she even looking for? Nine huffed in frustration, wishing she had never stepped foot inside this awful shop. The longer she spent in Beyond, the more she began to feel that shopping was overrated. Now here she was, dangling above the ground at a considerable height – she had no idea how high, but high enough to really not want to drop. The best thing to do was to observe, listen to her gut feelings, and – somehow – choose a secret...

And as she resigned herself to this fact, Nine felt her fingertips itch, just a little. Curiosity had always been Nine's curse as well as her blessing. She gazed at the jars, with their coloured letters swirling around inside. She couldn't read the words – everything was moving too fast and jumbled about. But it was a secret. Somebody's secret. Which one would she choose? What would she find out?

Despite everything, Nine felt a strange buzz of excitement. Her fingertips hovered thoughtfully and curiously over each jar, as if she were trying to sense the type of secret inside. The sparkling letters had said to trust her instincts, yet she didn't know what she was actually meant to be looking for.

Which to choose? Which to choose?

Then her keen eyes saw it. A tall, thin-necked bottle with a bulbous base. Bright turquoise letters swirled around inside. Something about the bottle drew her. She couldn't explain why.

Nine snatched up the bottle. "This secret," she said, surprised at how much her heart was thumping. She clasped the bottle tightly.

The sparkling ribbons floated back down through the blackness, until Nine's feet hit solid ground again. The ribbons unwrapped from her waist and faded into nothing.

THAT ONE?

ARE YOU SURE?

"Yes," said Nine, watching the turquoise letters swirling inside the bottle.

INTERESTING.

"That's it? I can just go?" asked Nine.

YES.

Nine turned to leave when the red sparkly letters appeared once more in the air.

BUT BE WARNED. THERE WILL BE ... CONSEQUENCES.

The letters faded away but Nine stood rooted to the spot. A chill was seeping through her bones. Because she knew those words. She knew that voice.

Oh no. Oh no. It couldn't be...

Stepping forward through the sparkling letters, which faded as she touched them, came a young woman with tumbling, scarlet hair, clad in an elaborate, black crinoline dress that merged with the darkness surrounding her. The woman had ancient eyes and flared nostrils and was someone Nine unfortunately knew too well.

Flabberghast's sister.

The one who had cursed the House at the Edge of Magic.

CHAPTER 13

Every muscle in Nine's body tensed.

"Oh, I've been watching you," said the witch. "Watching you for a *very* long time."

"I *knew* someone was following me!" Nine growled. "That was you, wasn't it? What do you want? What are you doing here?"

The witch gestured to the shop. "Oh, running a little business, revealing a few secrets, ruining a few lives." She smiled her dark and dangerous smile. "Having a little fun."

"I don't like it when you have fun," Nine said sourly.

The witch gave a tinkly laugh. She walked towards Nine, until there were only a couple of inches separating them. "Then you are terribly boring! Perhaps I should make life more *interesting* for you." She stared pointedly at Nine. "As I did for your mother."

Nine flinched at the mention of her ma but held the witch's gaze. "You knew my ma?"

"Oh, yes," said the witch, in her smooth voice. The witch extended her hand and held Nine's chin, examining her. Nine pulled herself free. "Don't say my brother neglected to tell you that?"

"Yes," Nine said tightly. "Funnily enough, he did leave that bit out."

The witch tutted. "He always ignores anything that makes him uncomfortable. Terrible at facing up to things, my foolish brother. He does so hate it when stories end badly."

Badly?

"But there's something he hasn't realised," said the witch, smiling sweetly. She leaned forwards and whispered in Nine's ear, "The story has not ended yet."

Nine pulled away and stared at Flabberghast's sister. Hate, confusion and concern flurried around inside her. There were so many emotions, Nine had no idea which was going to explode first.

"What did you do to my ma?" Nine growled.

The witch let out a tinkly little laugh that made Nine's blood freeze and boil at the same time.

"I'm not going to tell you," the witch replied in a sing-song voice. She eyed Nine. "Unless you have another very good secret to sell."

Nine narrowed her eyes. "I don't think so." She caught the half-smile on the witch's face as she moved back towards the door. She felt for the handle in the gloom and her hand clasped around it. "I'm not selling you anything," Nine said over her shoulder.

The doormat in front of her lit up with the blood-red letters:

YOU ALREADY HAVE. ENJOY YOUR SECRET.

Nine yanked on the handle and screwed her eyes up in pain at the light from outside. She stuffed her secret jar into her satchel, then shielded her eyes with her hand. She turned back around to look at the Secret Shop of Secrets...

But there was nothing there. Just the sound of an invisible door shutting behind her, followed by a distant, cold, tinkly laugh.

The candle poked open the flap of the satchel and the little flame popped up. "Ooh, she's a nasty bit of work and no mistake. She seems to know a lot about everything."

132

"Yes," said Nine, her mind buzzing as she marched back towards the House Park. "Too much."

"Ooh, but I can't wait for you to open this secret jar!" the candle prattled on. "Can I watch? Can I? Can I?"

"Ssshhh!" hissed Nine. "I've got more important things to think about than other people's silly secrets!" Her head was indeed filled with so many swirling thoughts, just like a secret trapped in a jar. She felt slightly sick. If the witch had known her ma, she had surely *done* something to her ma. And, knowing the witch, it wasn't something very pleasant—

THUD! Nine was taken aback as her knees crashed into something. She looked down and saw a disgruntled gargoyle.

"Oi! Watch where you goin'!" said Cas from somewhere underneath the massive hat that completely blocked her vision.

Nine reached over and pulled the hat from Cas's head. "Why don't *you*?" she snapped.

"Can't see with me hat on, can I?" Cas said.

"You don't even like hats!" Nine said grumpily.

"Mighta changed me mind."

Before Nine had the chance to reply, Bonehead strolled into view, still wearing his pink fluffy socks, and humming away. He twirled the parasol contentedly over his shoulder. The basket floated behind him, packed to overflowing with a miniature lamppost, a small pot plant with flimsy draping branches waving around like tentacles, the covered cage, a brass bed-warming pan, surely a lifetime's supply of pancake mix, and many other things that Nine didn't even recognise.

Bonehead's thin fingers wiggled with delight, and he plucked the cloth-covered cage from the shopping basket, which seemed to breathe a sigh of relief and float a little higher.

"Bonehead, that cage—"

"I know!" said the skeleton. "It's almost as thrilling as the socks."

Nine held her tongue. Although she couldn't tell from the skeleton's expression how happy he was, his little fluffy-socked bounce made it perfectly clear.

"Fine," said Nine with a sigh. "Look, we need to get back to the House. Dish and Spoon need to sort that formula before Ophidia turns up demanding her crockery back or we will all end up looking like Bonehead. Besides, I have a bone to pick with that wizard." She looked at the hundreds of houses. "Now, where did we park?"

There was a soft, distant BOOM. A sickly green smoke wavered above the houses.

"Never mind," said Nine, heading for the smoky trail. "Come on."

They made their way towards the House. Nine could hear Dish and Spoon arguing in muffled and distant voices from inside. Her heart sank. It didn't sound like finding the formula for Ophidia had gone particularly well.

"Oh dear," said Bonehead. "I believe we're doomed."

"You always believe we're doomed," grumbled Nine.

Flabberghast stood at the front door and ushered them in. He poked his head outside and looked around nervously, then swiftly shut the door behind them.

"You'll never guess who I've just bumped into. Your sister."

Flabberghast's eyes widened in dismay.

"She sends her love. You," said Nine, pointing her finger at Flabberghast, "didn't tell me she knew my ma."

"How did you…? Where did you—?" Flabberghast sneezed violently and glared at Cas's hat.

"That's what you've been keeping quiet. What did your sister do to her?"

"Madam," said Flabberghast, flushing red. "I do not know what you are talking about. All I know is that they were friends and then they were not – but this is no time for a lecture in family history! Make haste!" he said. "Once Gazillion has told my aunt that we've un-dish-napped Dish, she will be furious. She may appear at any moment, and we're not exactly ready!"

He grabbed the floating, struggling basket and dragged it a little way down the hallway.

"Where on earth you gonna put all that?" said Cas, peeping from under her hat as the wizard grabbed an armful of shopping from the basket.

Flabberghast ignored her question but moved towards the cupboard under the stairs, which bore a sign that read "NEVER OPEN THIS DOOR". He yanked it open.

"Leave the cage," Bonehead said, wagging a bony finger at the wizard, as Flabberghast shoved handfuls of shopping inside the cupboard. The basket shrank smaller and smaller as more and more stuff was removed.

They were friends and then they were not. Nine grabbed the pot plant before it was hurled inside

136

and prodded one of the waving tentacles. It slapped her hand lightly, then went on waving as if it was dancing to inaudible music.

"I want to know what happened," Nine said to Flabberghast's back as he continued to empty the shopping.

The wizard paused for a moment, then turned around and met Nine's eyes. "You may find, Madam, that some things are best left in shadow."

The basket was finally empty and back to the size of a matchbox. It zipped back down the hallway, repeatedly butting the door until Eric lumbered over to open it. Nine watched as the basket whizzed away in joyful freedom, presumably intending never to shop with them again.

Flabberghast rubbed his nose and reached for Cas's hat. "I told you ... not to ... ACHOO!"

"I'm keeping me hat," said Cas, lifting her head to peer out defiantly from underneath the brim.

Flabberghast pointed a finger at her and was opening his mouth to retort, when Spoon's frustrated voice floated down from the kitchen.

"One ingredient! Just one blasted ingredient missing from our formula!"

Nine sighed. She hated to admit it but Flabberghast was right. They had more pressing problems than discovering what had passed between her ma and Flabberghast's sister. She headed down the hallway. Eric came lolloping out of the kitchen and met her at the doorway, his eyes wide and relieved. "Lady back. Lady safe." He looked deep into Nine's eyes. "Lady fine?"

Nine took Eric's hand in her own, hoping the squeeze she gave it made up for everything. She hated herself for not trusting him with her ma's secret. Her own secret. And she hated herself even more for hurting the troll's feelings. "Lady fine."

Eric gave a wonky-tusky smile. Nine frowned as she peered past him and saw Dish and Spoon standing by the table in front of a large bowl of pink gloop. Both were covered with splats of the stuff, and each clutched half of a torn piece of paper.

"Oh dear!" cried Dish, wiping some pink gloop from her nose. "We have surely tried every ingredient with our halves of the formula. Why will it not turn gold? She wants gold, not *pink*."

"How – can – it – still – be – pink?" Spoon groaned, unsheathing his sword and stabbing the bowl of pink gloop with every word.

Nine slammed the pot plant on the table, then put her hands on her hips. "I've had enough secrets for one day. For one YEAR. Look – an angry, unpredictable aunt is due any moment wanting some serious answers and you still haven't managed to make not-exactly-gold. Will someone at least tell us what the not-exactly gold *actually* is?"

Everyone looked at Dish and Spoon.

Dish and Spoon looked at each other.

Spoon gave a loud sigh and flicked one of the pink blobs from his kilt. "It's just like gold, lass, unless you know what you're looking for."

"Why would she want fake gold?" said Nine.

"Professor Dish," demanded Flabberghast. "What *is* going on?"

"The material has a special property." Dish's cheeks began to blush. She looked at Spoon nervously. "It can magnify thought, memory, but more commonly ... power. It's called Stargold."

Flabberghast's mouth dropped open. "Surely the existence of Stargold is just a centuries-old tale told by Maudeline the Completely and Utterly Unreliable in her book *The Giant Snail Disaster of 1332*. She tells of a substance that magnifies power but at great cost to the one who wields it!"

He turned to look at Dish and Spoon. "It magnifies power" – the wizard tugged handfuls of his curly hair – "and *you're* planning to hand this over to Ophidia the Unpredictable? The most unstable, power-hungry witch in all the realms?!"

"We didn't know Gazillion was going to hand it over to Ophidia!" Dish protested. "Not until she tracked me down in impatience and trapped me in the This-And-That shop!"

"And all because you wanted to get your hands on a little bit of magic?"

"It was a mistake," said Dish, putting her hands where her hips would have been if she hadn't been a perfect circle shape. Her eyes became watery. "Gazillion was very persuasive. And all my years of experiments have brought me nothing but misery and failure. In truth, I have nothing to show for it. Have *you* never wanted something or done something just to prove your own worth? Never?"

Flabberghast looked hurt and was silent. Nine suspected, in his mind, he was replaying all the Hopscotch Championships he had ever taken part in and thinking again of his lack of magical powers. She had never thought of him as Flabberghast the Unworthy, but that was the name bestowed upon him.

"Anyway, we have no choice now, lad!" snapped

Spoon. "We only needed enough to make one blasted locket and we can't even get that right!"

"A locket?" said Nine.

The Secret Shop of Secrets. Mr Downes... The guilt came flooding back.

"That was what I was asked to make with the Stargold," said Dish miserably. "I guess it was so that Ophidia could carry it with her always. That's the kind of power you want to keep close to your chest."

Flabberghast nodded. "And I dread to think what will happen if we don't get it to her. She's got rather a history with lockets. You should have seen what she did to Uncle Mortimer the Unwise when he sold her favourite locket to the This-And-That Shop to pay for his ever-increasing Dragon Droppings collection." He grimaced at the memory. "Shall we just say it caused a considerable mess. In more ways than one."

"Your whole family is a considerable mess!" snapped Nine. "Speaking of which, you'll never guess *where* I bumped into your sister. The Secret Shop of Secrets."

"What? What is she doing there?" Flabberghast groaned again and sank into one of the kitchen chairs.

"A nice little trade by the looks of things." Nine said curtly, narrowing her eyes at the wizard.

Flabberghast thudded his head down onto the table, his arms dropping limply by his sides. "Why did she have to be here?"

"Never mind your flamin' sister!" said Spoon. "We've enough trouble with your aunt!"

"Why do they *both* have to be here?" moaned Flabberghast into the tabletop.

"I knew we were doomed," droned Bonehead, collapsing into a rattly-bony heap on a chair opposite him. "Not even fluffy socks can make up for being doomed."

"We are not doomed!" said Nine. "We just need to work out a way out of this situation caused by YOU, YOU, YOU!" She pointed to Flabberghast, Dish and Spoon.

"And probably YOU," giggled a high-pitched voice from Nine's satchel.

Nine froze. Dish and Spoon frowned. Nine let out a small cough, which she hoped sounded convincing. "Sorry, my throat is … funny."

"You should visit the apothecary, Madam," said Flabberghast, still face down, "and ask for a remedy."

Spoon pointed at Nine's satchel with the hand not holding parchment, opened his mouth to speak…

There was the sudden sound of insistent knocking on the door. Flabberghast lifted his head sharply from the table.

"Open the door, dear. Why don't we have a lovely cup of that lovely tea you mentioned?" came Ophidia's rich, spiky voice.

"If only Aunt Ophidia was a green-horned minotaur. I have just the remedy from the This-And-That Shop," said Flabberghast. He paused. "I think, on the whole, I'd prefer the minotaurs."

More knocking.

"Flabberghast, I must insist. Gazillion reports you have something of mine. And it would be a terrible shame if we fell out over this ... *dear.*"

There was the sound of a sharp-heeled shoe kicking the door.

"Flabberghast the Unworthy!" screeched Ophidia. "Open this door at once, you wretched boy! That dish is mine!"

But then the kicking stopped.

"She gone?" asked Eric, looking at Nine with his wide eyes.

"If she has," said Nine, "I bet it won't be for long."

"Strawberry tea," gasped Flabberghast as he hurried down the hallway to the kitchen. "If my aunt does get in, we'll need to pacify her. There's nothing better than the Finest Tea in All the Realms for calming the soul. Eric, put the kettle on and fetch the teapot." The wizard was reaching for the tea cupboard when a strange rattling came from the arched door on the right-hand side of the kitchen.

"Is it the Sometimes Dead waking up? Because that really isn't going to help us right now," said Nine, feeling every muscle in her body tensing. The Sometimes Dead were Flabberghast's relatives who didn't exactly *live* in the crypt because they were dead – but had a tendency to wander about from time to time.

Eric backed away from the door in alarm and promptly collided with the bucket that collected the orange gloop which dripped from the ceiling. "Oops!" he cried, his mouth downturned, as the teapot flew from his hands and smashed on the floor. His long-nailed hands flew to his cheeks. "Poor teapot!"

Everyone else watched as the bucket went flying across the kitchen, sending orange gloop hurtling in Dish and Spoon's direction. With a stomach-churning SPLAT, a pea-sized glob of orange gloop splattered onto the tiny pink patch still on Spoon's kilt.

"Oooh, my!" said Bonehead.

"The pink!" cried Dish. "It's turning gold."

Of course! When she had thrown the bucket of gloop over the man-eating Starflower in the conservatory once before, it had changed the petals to a golden colour.

"I don't think it's just changing colour," said Nine, staring in disbelief. "Something's happening!"

"As it's meant to!" breathed Dish. "I think that means…"

The gold was now sparking, fizzing on Spoon's kilt – as if the orange gloop had triggered a reaction with the other ingredients, woken up from a deep sleep and was now very much alive. Spoon had frozen, not looking pleased that something very much alive was fizzing on his kilt.

A little shiver ran down Nine's spine. The strange combination of ingredients had created something. Was this the Stargold?

But Nine didn't have time to ask, as, with a magnificent WHOOSH, a stream of glittering emerald fragments came shooting forcefully through the keyhole and landed on the brick-paved floor. The tiny green pieces swiftly built up from the ground, layering glitter upon glitter, until they took form.

The form of an extremely furious aunt.

CHAPTER 14

"Ah, Auntie Ophidia," said Flabberghast, in a voice that was at least an octave too high. "How nice of you to drop by. We were just putting the kettle on."

Ophidia narrowed her cold, purple eyes. "Your sister told me you had missed out the steps at the back of the House in your protection spell. You really should fix the spell, dear."

"Apparently so," said Flabberghast, tight-lipped.

"Oh, but you have no magic, do you? Such an embarrassing display at the Hopscotch Championship," continued Ophidia, strutting closer. "An utter disgrace."

Ophidia swished her emerald cloak behind her as her high heels clicked menacingly on the brick floor. She loomed over Dish, whose little mouth dropped open in alarm. The hand holding the parchment began to shake a little.

"Run!" shouted Nine to Spoon, who grabbed Dish's other hand and headed for the kitchen door.

"Oh, I don't think so," said Ophidia. There was a twist of her wrist, and green strands flew out, slamming the door shut.

Dish and Spoon exchanged a worried glance and looked down at their pieces of parchment, then at Ophidia. Spoon moved his parchment over the fizzing gold blob on his kilt.

"Doomed, I tell you!" moaned Bonehead.

"You can't leave Beyond yet," said Nine, squaring up to Ophidia. "You can't have done all your shopping. The bookshop still isn't open."

Ophidia strutted slowly towards Dish and Spoon and towered over them. "Well, while I'm waiting, I can deal with you, Professor."

"Oh, Miss Ophidia, we've made brilliant progress," said Dish, moving in front of Spoon and holding up her piece of parchment.

Ophidia narrowed her eyes at Spoon. "*We?*"

Dish looked at Spoon in panic.

Flabberghast dashed across the kitchen, his hand outstretched. "Tea cupboard!" he called.

ZAP! Ophidia was a tiny jack-in-the-box with fluffy hair and a long nose that reached down to the ground. Nine was a jar of secrets balanced precariously on the top of a broom handle. Flabberghast grew taller and bumped the ceiling. Eric sprouted wings and a beak. Bonehead's bones all disconnected and whirled around, chasing each other in a large circle. Cas turned a funny shade of purple, then laid an egg. Dish turned into a bubble and floated towards the table. And Spoon became a giant blob of fizzing, sparkling gold. There was silence for a moment, then the jar-of-secrets-Nine overbalanced on the broom handle, smashed onto the floor, and turned back into normal Nine.

Nine shook herself back to her senses and looked around at the others as they returned to normal.

"Forgive me, Aunt," gabbled Flabberghast, as he shrank back down to regular wizard size and Ophidia's long nose vanished, "but I'm sure you will appreciate a cup of tea. Ah. Except..." He looked sadly at the smashed teapot.

Ophidia marched over to Spoon and held him in the air by one of his spindly arms. As the parchment dangled from his hand, she stared at his kilt, her eyes wide. Spoon tried in vain to reach for his sword.

"You put me down right now, or so help me, I'll—"

But Ophidia ignored him. Her eyes sparkled silver with joy as, with her finger, she scraped the golden gloop from his kilt. She flicked it into the air where it solidified and floated, glinting mischievously in a way that somehow made Nine feel rather nervous. Ophidia shot a single thread of sparkling emerald from one of her fingertips. It touched the solidified not-exactly-gold in the air and—

BOOM! There was an explosion of emerald that rocked the House, causing Bonehead's bones to rattle as green drops rained down all over the kitchen. Eric leaned over Nine, protecting her from the droplets. A few seconds later, Nine released the breath she hadn't realised she was holding. She peeked out from Eric's bark-like arms to see Ophidia trying to catch her breath for a moment, then the older witch threw back her curly, white-haired head and laughed.

"I am so thrilled," gabbled Flabberghast, looking as delighted as a dead slug. "Although might I suggest you save that lovely yet slightly shocking trick for special events. Birthdays. Momentous deaths. That kind of thing."

"And that is with one tiny drop, boy!" whooped Ophidia. "Wait until I have enough for a locket!"

Her eyes glinted dangerously. "Then watch me put those who oppose me in their place. Starting with my sister."

Flabberghast gulped. "Auntie Griselda? I agree that on the whole sisters are undoubtedly more trouble than they are worth but—"

She threw her arms wide dramatically. "Too long have I tolerated the backbiting and the power-stealing. I have bided my time, and soon I shall show my sister and every living soul what I truly am."

"The most unstable, power-hungry witch in all the realms?" Nine said sharply. Ophidia whirled to face her and opened her mouth to speak, but Flabberghast dashed forward, his hands nervously outstretched to guide his aunt out of the kitchen.

"Well, this has been marvellous, Auntie. We shall reschedule the tea party when we have a new teapot – which, who knows, could possibly take years! Now, you do not want to miss the bookshop—"

Ophidia spun around to him, twisted her wrist, and green strands taped themselves over his mouth. Flabberghast's eyes grew wide, and his hands dashed to his face.

"Silence, foolish boy," she barked.

"Well, I finally have what I am owed," Ophidia

said, turning to Dish and Spoon with a laugh that made Nine shiver. She held out a green-fingernailed hand expectantly. "Hand over the formula."

"The..." began Dish cautiously. "The magical gift I was promised?"

Ophidia threw back her head and laughed. "Come, now! You do not seriously believe *you* were going to receive a powerful magical gift?" She snatched the parchment from both Dish and Spoon.

"I was promised!" cried Dish.

Spoon's moustache bristled furiously and he drew his sword from its sheath. Ophidia shook her head. "And you believed it. That is *your* problem." She narrowed her purple eyes. "And I have a rather regrettable problem of my own. I have access to the formula" – she waved the papers she was holding – "but so do you two."

Spoon and Dish stared at each other, their little mouths gaping open in shock and surprise.

"And we can't have that now," continued Ophidia, tucking the formula parchments inside her cloak. "Can we?"

A sick feeling of panic shot through Nine, but before she could speak or move, emerald sparks once more shot from Ophidia's fingertips, this time towards

Dish and Spoon. With the quickest of zaps, he became a rigid, motionless, ordinary spoon. His little face disappeared, and his spindly arms and legs shrank back into the handle. Dish's face disappeared, her arms and legs vanishing back into the bowl of the dish. She spun round on her side from the power of the blast, until finally the lifeless dish toppled onto the floor.

"No!" cried Nine. She stared in shock.

How – how could she? How dare she?

"I could use a new bowl," Ophidia said, snatching up the dish, "for my pet fang-toothed worms to eat from." Dish and Spoon both shrank in size until they fitted in the palm of her hand. Then she stuffed them inside her cloak.

"You – you can't! You change them back!" pleaded Nine, pointing her finger furiously at Ophidia, tears prickling behind her eyes.

"Oh, spare them your pity, mortal! You play with fire, you prepare to be burned," Ophidia said bluntly. "It was their choice. And their mistake to accept the commission." She click-clacked over to Flabberghast and pinched his cheek. "Gorgeous to see you, dear. I'll see myself out."

Then she stepped back, and, before anyone could move, Ophidia threw open her arms and burst into a thousand glittery green pieces, which whooshed over to the fireplace and shot up the chimney.

"Your aunt! How could she?" raged Nine.

"She is not called 'the Unpredictable' for nothing," said Flabberghast, as the green threads taped across his mouth disappeared. His face looked like he had just eaten one of Eric's pancakes.

Nine glanced at the troll, who was still staring down at the broken teapot. Then he looked at Nine. "Spoon gone?" he said sadly. "Liked Spoon. Spoon friend."

His words pushed Nine into action. "Come on!" she said. "We can't let her take Spoon and Dish!"

"She already has!" Cas argued. "I don't fancy me chances against the likes of her! And as she said, their foolish choice. Don't see why my head should roll to save 'em. This ain't what I signed up for when I came with you to travel the realms. Not sure this is the life for me. I say we visit the bookshop and get out of here."

"Madam," said Flabberghast, his shoulders slumped. "I fear there is little we *can* do. Anyone who gets involved with my aunt does so at their peril. My aunt is a very powerful witch even without the Stargold. If we chased her down, we would not possibly have the strength to fight her, and I do not have my wretched magic to even attempt to

153

change them back! I wish above all that I did!" His eyes filled with tears of defeat. "My companions are my family."

"Well, this has all rather spoiled the mood. I suppose I shall go back to the closet," said Bonehead gloomily, pushing his chair back. "For ever."

But fire and fury and frustration burned inside Nine. She looked at her defeated companions, and the shattered teapot. "Maybe *you* can't help…" she said, as an idea lit up in her mind.

Should she?

Did she dare?

Oh, this is surely the worst idea ever in all the realms…

"Lady plan?" asked Eric, looking a little nervous. He cradled the handle and spout of the teapot, looking at her with wide yellow eyes.

But what other choice is there?

"Lady plan," said Nine decidedly. She looked at Flabberghast. "Will you trust me?"

Flabberghast stared at Nine, the swirl of frustration, sadness and defeat clear in his eyes. He swallowed hard. "Yes, Madam. I trust you."

Nine gave the briefest smile in return.

"But what…?"

Nine wasn't interested in more questions and, without giving anyone the chance to stop her, she ran from the kitchen, down the hallway, casting the briefest of glances at the cloth-covered cage, and to the front door, ignoring the voices behind her.

"Lady wait!"

No.

"Madam!"

No.

"We are definitely doomed!"

No.

"Oh blimey. Anyone thought about lockin' 'er up?"

Quite probably.

But nothing would make Nine stop. She ran from the House and darted through the House Park, heading towards the town. Dodging through the colourful witches and wizards and their numerous floating shopping baskets. Past the towering grid of the hopscotch sports shop, the giant plant pot, and the open snaky mouth of the Pest Shop. On she ran, thinking how life had been simpler when it was just her alone, pickpocketing to survive. She would never have done what she was about to do. Yes, it had been simpler then, easier... But now life was more complicated. And more beautiful.

As she darted down the cobbled streets of Beyond, she thought of Spoon and everything they had been through together – if there was any chance, *any chance*, she could do *anything...* Flabberghast trusted her to make the best decision, and this was the best she had, so on she ran.

Until she reached the last visible building.

The bookshop.

Nine stopped and caught her breath. Unable to resist, she ran up the bookish steps to the front door. The sign beside it read "OPEN IN TEN MINUTES", then faded and changed to "REALLY REALLY PROMISE THIS TIME." Nine turned down the side of the bookshop, pushing away the desperate desire to break into it somehow and discover what her ma had left for safekeeping. She turned away from the bookshop and instead, Nine walked on down the side, with her hands outstretched. She scrabbled for the door handle, twisted it angrily and threw the invisible door open. She marched into the blackness, fists clenched, ready for a fight, as the word "SHHH" appeared on the doormat in blood-red letters, then vanished again.

The front door clicked quietly behind her, encasing her in darkness.

For a moment, the only sound was Nine's heartbeat, which pounded away in her ears.

Then the scarlet words appeared one by one.

FANCY

SEEING

YOU.

Nine threw forward her arm, and swished impatiently at the sparkling words, causing them to vanish.

This is stupid. This is dangerous. This is absolutely the only thing I can think of.

The witch appeared out of the darkness, her cascade of red hair framing her smirking, threatening face.

Nine tried to control the shake in her voice, as she looked the witch straight in her ancient, blue eyes. "I'm here," she said, "to do a deal."

OUR LITTLE SECRET

CHAPTER 15

The witch threw back her head and laughed her tinkly laugh. Then her head snapped back down and she looked Nine dead in the eye. Her smile vanished instantly, and her eyes were cold.

"And what is it that you desire so badly, dearest thief, that you come to me for help?"

The words stung Nine. Help. She hated asking for help at the best of times, and this was most certainly *not* the best of times.

"You're the only one who can stop Ophidia," Nine said, forcing out the words. "She's changed Dish and Spoon into a normal dish and spoon and—"

"Boring!" sang the witch. "I have no interest in them whatsoever."

Nine tried hard to stay calm. "Spoon is your brother's friend!"

The witch began strutting around Nine in a threatening circle, examining a scarlet fingernail. "My brother? Dear oh dear, little thief, you really will have to try much harder than this. Family is highly overrated."

The floodgates holding back Nine's frustration could not take much more. "They're making a formula for Stargold. You must have heard of Stargold! Ophidia has the formula now!" *Minus an ingredient but that's my little secret.*

"You can take it, make the Stargold and be the most powerful witch in the realms!" Nine tried not to think about what that could mean.

"I do not need alchemy for that!" hissed the witch, still circling Nine. "A formula for Stargold is not what I desire."

The floodgates burst. "Then what?" Nine yelled, the fear and frustration exploding out of her. She put her hands on her hips. "There must be something you care about besides yourself!"

For the briefest moment, Nine saw a flicker of something in the witch's eyes – sadness? Pain? But as quickly as Nine noticed it, the moment had passed.

The witch stopped circling Nine and stood right in front of her.

"That is my business," said the witch. She narrowed her eyes at Nine. "My aunt is foolish for desiring that formula. I have my sights on something else. Something far more interesting. Something, as it happens, little thief, only you" – the witch twisted a wrist and red threads shot from her fingertips, grabbing Nine by the chin and tilting her face upwards to meet the witch's gaze – "can help me with."

"What?" said Nine, rubbing her chin as the threads released their grip and faded away.

"Shhh!" said the witch, flashing her dangerous smile once more. "Secrets."

"But you have to tell me what you want me to do!"

The witch tutted and shook her head. "And where is the fun in that? All you need to know is that it will require travelling through the World Between Worlds. Unfortunately, I find myself without a magical house."

"I thought you lived with your other aunt."

"Yeeeees," said the witch slowly. "Griselda the Unruly and I parted ways, after a most unfortunate argument that escalated somewhat." She sighed dramatically then smiled sweetly. "I'm sure she'll escape her wardrobe eventually. And I should prefer not to be around when she does. So," she continued lightly, "I find myself with a need to travel but lacking transportation. But I believe that's easily fixed. Do you not?"

The penny dropped, followed swiftly by Nine's jaw. "Travel with us? Flabberghast will never let you in the House!" She smirked slightly at the witch. "Family is highly overrated."

"Perhaps *he* will not let me in." The witch's eyes danced with mischief. "But *you* will."

Nine felt her heart sink to her toes. What on earth was she doing, asking the witch for help? Could she really let the witch travel with the House? Flabberghast would be beyond furious. He had made it perfectly clear he did not want her in his life.

Anything but this...

"It would be our little secret," whispered the witch. "It must be our little secret."

There is nothing but this...

Nine scowled. Oh, she hated this witch with every fibre of her body. But Flabberghast trusted Nine to help save Spoon and there was no other way.

"Fine!" she snapped, regret piercing her even as she spoke the word. "You get back Dish and Spoon, you can travel in the House."

"Then there remains just one problem, little thief," said the witch, circling her. She leaned forwards and whispered in Nine's ear. "How do I know I can trust you?"

"Me?" gasped Nine indignantly. "I'm not the one who curses houses and tricks people!"

"Yet you steal, little thief. You lie. And you betray." The witch raised an eyebrow. "The locket you stole. The candle in the satchel. Of course, I'm *certain* my brother knows you are speaking with me here." The witch smiled sweetly. "Shall I go on?"

Nine scowled. "Well, how do I know that I can trust *you*?"

The witch let out another tinkly laugh. "Oh, dearest thief. You know so very little. Do you remember what I told you the first time I met you? I told you that I was a friend."

"Oh yes, that's right. Just before you tried to kill me, wasn't it?" Nine said pointedly. "For your information, friends don't threaten each other with consequences."

"Oh," said the witch airily and smiled, "you'd be surprised."

Nine realised how little she actually knew about the witch standing in front of her, the one she was trusting to keep her word. "I don't even know your name."

"And I, dearest thief, don't even know yours... Not your real name. But then, neither do you, *Nine*."

The words stung. She had only ever known the name that the old gang-master had given her as the ninth orphan to join the gang.

"So we find ourselves in an unmovable position," said the witch, continuing to circle. "Perhaps we should both ... take a risk. Agreed?"

Nine stared at the witch with hatred and frustration as she strutted around her. What choice did she have? "Agreed," she growled.

Suddenly the witch stepped backwards and clapped her hands. "Well, the deal is done. How terribly exciting. Our little secret." There was that same flicker of sadness in the witch's eyes for the briefest of moments. Then it was gone.

Doubts and worries twisted inside Nine, but she was determined to show the witch no weakness. "Fine. Play your games! Now, we need to stop Ophidia. But we don't even know where she is!"

"Ah," said the witch, "but we do know exactly where she will be. You cannot leave Beyond without buying or trading something from each shop. What is the one shop that has not yet opened?"

"The bookshop."

"Gather your pathetic friends. I believe, dearest thief, it is time to go shopping. And when you have finished in the bookshop, I do not care how you achieve it, but you must bring my aunt here. I will be waiting for her."

The witch gave yet another tinkly laugh. "And so, the game truly begins."

Then she stepped backwards into the shadows of the shop and vanished from view. Before Nine's eyes, the red sparkly letters reappeared.

OUR LITTLE SECRET.

Back outside, Nine squinted at the daylight and ran back to the House Park. Everything felt so confusing and horrible. She felt so lost – so completely and utterly bewildered. Had she made the right decision? Was she right to make a deal with the witch? It was a risk she had to take. But there was something even worse...

She reached the House, slamming the front door behind her.

"Madam?" came Flabberghast's concerned voice from the kitchen.

What was even worse was that Nine had discussed matters with his archenemy. Done a deal with her. She felt she had betrayed his trust and hoped with all her heart he'd understand that this was the only way.

"Lady back?"

Nine ignored their voices. She didn't want to talk. Not to Flabberghast, not to Eric, not to anyone. She would absolutely bet that if she did betray the witch and told Flabberghast what had happened, his sister would somehow find out. She always seemed to know so much. About everyone. About everything. Nine suspected the Secret Shop of Secrets had a lot to do with this.

Nine reached the top of the plum-carpeted stairs and arrived at the landing. She hardly registered that she'd climbed the rickety flight of stairs, leading to a silvery door that was decorated with a golden question mark.

Nine opened the door and breathed in the faintly familiar scent of her mother's room. She just needed to be there, for a moment, desperate for comfort before she led her friends into danger. She wished with all her heart that her mother were here to

165

advise her. To guide her. To hold her and say that, somehow, everything would be all right. Because at the moment, it all felt messier than the cupboard under the stairs.

But her ma wasn't here. She would never be here again. Nine took off her satchel and plonked it beside the bed, then threw herself face down onto the soft, mauve quilt, narrowly missing *The Mystery of Wolven Moor.*

"Hey!" said the candle from the satchel, pinned underneath Nine. "Don't forget about me!"

Nine rolled over and pulled out the candle. "Sorry," she said, standing it on the little wooden bedside table.

"Ooh, you've got yourself in a right old pickle, haven't you?" gasped the candle, with wide eyes in its little flame. "Those friends of yours downstairs are going to be right cross with you when they find out! 'Specially that one with the curly hair and the pointy hat. He really doesn't like his sister, does he?"

Nine frowned but the candle just kept going.

"Still, least you can keep a secret. You know, I'm rubbish at it – I can't seem to stop talking. I just want to be useful but everyone takes me back to the shop time and time again and—"

Nine leaned over and blew the candle out. The candle huffily puffed a little wisp of smoke out of its wick and reignited itself.

"Rude. I just want to be useful," it muttered.

KNOCKITY-KNOCK.

The candle quickly extinguished itself a split second before Flabberghast burst inside. "Madam, what is your plan for rescuing Dish and Spoon? We're waiting!"

"We need to go to the bookshop as soon as we can," said Nine, rubbing her face with her hands. "It promises it will be open any minute. Your aunt will visit, too, and you need to reason with her."

And I'll try to find what my ma left...

"Reason with her?!" snorted Flabberghast. "Have you ever tried to reason with someone called 'the Unpredictable'? I'd stand more chance of persuading the Sometimes Dead to tidy the cupboard under the stairs!" He frowned. "Although, my sister did manage to get them to do that once. I trust you've not bumped into her again?"

Nine swallowed hard, hating the lie she forced onto her tongue. "No."

Flabberghast nodded. "That is some good fortune, at least. Far better our paths never cross again. This is

167

all the plan you have? I fear it is a dangerous move."

Nine nodded, trying to stop the confession from spilling out. *Well, we won't be by ourselves.*

"I just need you to trust me," Nine said quietly. "It's the only way to save … our family."

Flabberghast looked at Nine and sighed. "Madam, you are stubborn, hot-headed, inquisitive beyond tolerance, but" – the silvery sparkles appeared in his eyes – "I would trust you with my life. And I hope you would do the same."

Nine swallowed hard. Would she trust Flabberghast with her life? With everything?

RECEIVED WITH THANKS, THE SAFEKEEPER.

Flabberghast cleared his throat and his gaze caught the candle on the bedside table. "Ah, at least you bought a candle for my study. That will come in useful."

He walked over and picked it up.

"Oh," said Nine, trying to snatch the candle back. "Um – no, I really don't think you should…"

"What, Madam?"

Nine's heart sank. More lies. More deception. More mistakes.

"Nothing," she said, and released her grip on the candle. Her heart sank even lower as she saw the candle briefly ignite, its overjoyed face giving her a wink behind Flabberghast's back as he moved towards the door. "I'll tell the others the plan."

Well, part of the plan...

Everything inside Nine just wanted to burst.

"Flabberghast?" she called out, making the wizard stop in the doorway and look around. "I'm... I'm sorry."

Flabberghast frowned. "Madam? Sorry for what?"

"For..." Nine hesitated. "For the way everything has worked out."

The wizard looked confused for a moment, then left the room.

Nine pulled the jar out of her satchel and stared at the swirling turquoise letters – the secret – inside. It was impossible to make out any words. She placed it on the table beside the bed. She put her hand on the cork lid, to release the secret ... then moved her hand away. She would listen to it later. There was no room in her head for someone else's thoughts – it was too full of her own.

There was one last chance at the bookshop.

One last chance to save Dish and Spoon.

And every chance that it was going to go horribly wrong.

CHAPTER 16

It was a nervous cohort of companions that waited by the front door. A skeleton with slumped shoulders and pink fluffy socks, a grumpy gargoyle who still insisted on wearing the oversized hat, a tail-wringing troll who turned and looked at Nine with worried eyes as she came downstairs, and a downcast wizard holding his arm out to the umbrella stand by the front door. The strange blue arm, as always, whizzed out holding the wizard's cloak. It felt odd and empty without Spoon there, waving his sword and commanding the charge.

"Right," said Flabberghast, as he opened the front door. "We go to the bookshop. We confront my aunt. We demand the return of Dish and Spoon, our true family—"

"And we all get turned into stone!" muttered Cas.

"You're already stone," said Nine.

"Stonier stone," said Cas.

"Friends, this may be our final battle," said Flabberghast solemnly. "A fight we cannot overcome. A battle we cannot win. A destiny we cannot escape. A—"

"Oh, come *on*! Let's go!" snapped Nine and pushed past him. She grabbed Eric's hand and pulled him along beside her.

The girl, the wizard, the troll, the gargoyle and the skeleton marched across the House Park, through the town, until they stood outside the bookshop.

Nine looked around. There was no sign of Ophidia, and no sign of Flabberghast's sister. Nine couldn't decide if this was good news or not. Nine glanced towards the invisible door of the Secret Shop of Secrets. Was the witch in there still? Waiting for Nine to keep her part of the arrangement and lead the others in? *Into what? A trap?*

"Bookshop scary," said Eric, looking at the front door.

"Eric is not incorrect," said Flabberghast. "Now, listen. I must warn you."

"Warn?" Nine narrowed her eyes.

"The shopkeeper left suddenly some years ago."

"Yes, I know," Nine said impatiently.

"Oh," said Flabberghast, looking puzzled. "How did you know that?"

Nine kicked herself, as she thought of the candle. "Must have just heard it somewhere. Anyway, why *did* he leave?"

"Nobody knows, Madam. Most mysterious. A pleasant fellow, I recall. You'll see him when you leave the shop. He set up a spell of his image to bid farewell to his customers." He frowned. "That particular spell is fine, but heed my warning, Madam. He left other spells for the bookshop to keep running in his absence. Regretfully, over time, some of them have become a little lazy and … mutated."

"Mutated?!" said Nine, whirling around to face Flabberghast. "Is this bookshop going to try to kill us? This had better not be that wretched library in the House all over again."

"Nonsense, Madam," said Flabberghast, but his voice was deadly serious. "To every customer that enters, it tries to sell the perfect book."

"Oh. And … why is that a bad thing?" said Nine.

"Because, Madam," said Flabberghast, "the bookshop is going to try *extremely* hard."

Suddenly, the blind on the door rolled up at lightning speed, making everyone jump.

"We find the books as quickly as we can, then we will be ready to deal with my aunt when she arrives. You must buy the book you are recommended, or we will never get out!"

"Never get out?!"

"Oh! And as there is no shopkeeper, you must pay the honesty box before you find your book," said Flabberghast, as he handed out some yonders to everyone. "It's gone a little bit ... rogue. Just grin and bear it." He looked pointedly at Nine. "And no arguing."

"What do you mean, 'no arguing'?"

The door creaked open.

"Welcome! Welcome!" said a voice that sounded slightly frazzled and exasperated. Nine's ears pricked up, and her heart skipped a beat, but she didn't know why. Before she had time to think about it, Flabberghast ushered them in towards a wooden honesty box that hovered in the air in front of them.

"Allow me to demonstrate," said Flabberghast, holding up his coin. He looked at Nine. "No arguing," he repeated, then dropped his coin into the honesty box.

173

"Good grief," said the box, as the coin slot moved like a mouth. "Look at the state of you. No magic? Better start at the beginning again. You seriously need to sort your life out, mate."

Flabberghast bit his tongue. "I'm ... working on it," he hissed. "If we could skip the counselling and just move swiftly on to the book recommendation, please."

"*Wizardry for Complete Beginners Who Are Utterly Terrible and Awful and—*"

"I get the message," snapped Flabberghast.

"By Oligant the Inexperienced."

Nine couldn't help a little snort but Flabberghast huffed very loudly. "Thank you so much," he said in a very clipped voice.

Eric dropped a coin into the box.

"Your pancakes are terrible, mate," said the box, its coin slot poking out a tongue. "Absolutely terrible."

Nine glared at the honesty box as Eric's face fell. "Oi," she said.

"Don't you worry, mate. I'm here to help. I can recommend the perfect book for you! Brand new, published only last week: *Perfect Pancakes* by Priscilla the Immaculate."

Eric's face lit up. "Eric pancakes! Nice pancakes!"

Cas dropped a coin into the slot and pushed her

174

hat back to glare at the box. "An' don't you be tellin' me that I'm too short or so help me, I'll knock your block off."

"Oh no, it's not that. YOU need to relax, mate. You're waaaay too uptight. Try a bubble bath."

"A bubble—?!"

"I recommend: *Relaxation for Unsuccessful or Retired Gargoyles* by Scabarella the Annoyingly Unflappable."

"I ain't unsuccessful or retired! I'm just … currently unemployed."

"Just get the book," growled the honesty box, as Flabberghast grabbed Cas's arm and pulled her away.

Nine looked around nervously as Bonehead dropped in his coin. Still no sign of Ophidia.

"Oh for goodness' sake," said the honesty box. "Look at you with your slumped shoulders! Come on, mate! Stand up straight! You'll put your hipbone out."

Bonehead suddenly straightened, jiggling rather guiltily. "It's not easy, you know. I've been dead for years, not that anyone cares—"

"*Positive Thinking for Brainless Skeletons* by Agnes the Twice Undead. Next!"

Nine stood in front of the box, dropped in her coin, and raised a defiant eyebrow.

"Not a word, remember!" called Flabberghast from near by. "We don't have time, Madam! We need to hurry and find our books!"

"Go on, then," said Nine, narrowing her eyes at the honesty box and folding her arms.

The honesty box tutted. "You, mate, need to be a bit more like me."

"What?" said Nine, frowning. "What do you mean?"

"Honest."

Nine's eyes widened, and she glanced over at the others in alarm. They looked back, confused.

"Knew it," said the honesty box, with a condescending sigh. "Got guilt written all over your face, mate! What've you done? Stolen something? Told a lie?" Its voice dropped to a whisper. "Betrayed someone?"

Nine could feel her cheeks flushing, her chest tightening. "Shut up!" she hissed urgently. "I've done nothing!"

"Aha! There you go again! Lies, lies, more lies!"

"Shut up!" said Nine. "Just give me my book recommendation."

Flabberghast marched over, frowning. "Madam, what in the name of strawberry tea is going on?"

176

"Nothing," Nine said, refusing to look him in the eye.

"She's lying," whispered the honesty box.

"About what?" demanded Flabberghast.

"Ooh," said the box, "I'd say pretty much everything."

"Now look here," said Flabberghast, "we're in a rush. You've had your payment, spoken your mind, now give my friend the book recommendation."

My friend...

The words were precious and beautiful but instead of warming Nine's heart, they broke it. Friends did not betray friends.

If he only knew.

"Book recommendation," said the honesty box, "is *The Mystery of Wolven Moor* by Horatio Piddlewick." The honesty box gasped. "What? I didn't mean to say that. No, that book can't be right. You need to learn to tell the truth. I recommend to you—" It made a strange gurgling sound as if it was fighting with its own tongue. "*The* ... gah! ... *Mystery of* ... gah! ... *Wolven Moor*," it said in a defeated and miserable voice.

"Of all the books, it has recommended one from your own world," murmured Flabberghast. "The

177

shopkeeper cast the spell to accurately recommend the perfect book for each customer. Even the honesty box, with its OVERRATED and HIGHLY INACCURATE opinions, cannot overrule that."

"I heard that," said the honesty box.

"I don't need that book. I've already got that book," Nine retorted.

"Buy another copy," growled the honesty box.

Flabberghast pulled her away. "Just do as it says. It cannot help but be honest. And as much as I hate to admit it, the recommendations are usually rather … beneficial. Make haste, Madam." He gave Nine a strange look, full of confusion and hurt.

Nine's heart burned. *Thief. Liar. Traitor.*

Then Flabberghast looked away. "We must find our books before Ophidia comes. We will not want to be battling both her and the bookshop at the same time!"

"Battling the bookshop?"

"Fear not, Madam. You'll get the hang of it."

Nine looked around as she went. Bundles of books crammed into every corner, on shelves, dangling from the ceiling… And somewhere here was something secret, hidden and left by her ma. She didn't have the foggiest clue where to start. How could you look for something when you didn't know what you were looking for?

They passed Eric, who had trundled off towards the right-hand side of the shop where a sign hanging from the wonky-beamed ceiling said "COOKERY".

"Eric book?" he mumbled to himself. He wrung his tail nervously as he scanned the shelves.

"You don't want pancakes," insisted a voice. "Biscuits. You want biscuits. The best biscuits in the realms."

"Eric pancake," mumbled Eric, not sounding very convincing.

"Stew! He wants stew!" came another voice. "Buy me! ME!"

"No, he wants pancakes!" called a third.

Nine stared in amazement as, suddenly, several books leapt from the cookery shelves.

"Here we go," Flabberghast sighed, then he called to Eric, "Don't give in! It has to be pancakes! You can do it!"

Nine gawped as some of the books seemed to be involved in a physical fight with each other in the air, frantically flapping their covers and pages at each other menacingly. Then a plate of biscuits appeared right under Eric's nose. His eyes widened and he clasped his hands over his mouth, and shook his head. Nine could actually smell the biscuits, freshly baked. Her mouth watered.

"Can I get one?" she said to Flabberghast. "Just one?"

"Certainly not!" said Flabberghast. "You'll only encourage them. The sales spell was meant to help the books showcase themselves, but it's all gone dangerously wrong. The books simply do not stop!" He pulled Nine further into the shop. "Pancakes!" he yelled to Eric.

Nine looked over her shoulder as a large bowl of stew and a ladle appeared from nowhere.

"See? Try it! Try it!" shouted the stew book, as the ladle plunged into the stew and emptied itself over Eric's head.

"PANCAKES!" Flabberghast yelled over his shoulder, as he dragged Nine onwards. But she stopped and looked in amazement, to see the whole shop exploding with frantic activity. Books flapping and flying and yelling. Different items were popping out of nowhere, desperately showcasing the content of the books.

Bonehead clattered by in his fluffy socks at an incredible speed.

"I'm doomed!" he yelled as he sprinted past, chased by about half a dozen positive thinking books lying on their side, frantically snapping themselves open and shut like vicious jaws, bellowing words of encouragement to him.

"Say to yourself, 'I am beautiful! Beautiful!' Now buy ME!"

"If you tell yourself you can do it," another shouted over the din, "YOU CAN DO IT! You hear me? YOU! CAN! DO! IT!"

"Help!" wailed Bonehead as his bony legs darted up the spiralling staircase to the next floor, with the deadly army of positive books snapping at his skull and encouraging him all the way.

"Get that out of your mouth!" Flabberghast yelled, pointing at Eric. The troll spun around, his mouth hastily closing around what appeared to be a double chocolate muffin, and his wide, yellow eyes shifting guiltily from side to side. "PAN-CAKES!"

Nine stared. "This is chaos!"

There was a sudden sploshing sound as Cascadia came whooshing by on a flood of lavender-scented bubbles which carried her across the shop floor, surrounded by several books. The warm water beneath the bubbles rushed around their knees.

"I can't swim! I can't swim!" wailed Cas, as she was swept along, clutching her hat in one hand.

"Worrying solves nothing," said one of the books in a soothing voice. "Just breathe in—"

"AAAARGHHHH!" said Cas, as she crashed into a wobbly, ceiling-high pile of books and brought the whole astronomy section crashing down. Stars and planets darted out of the books and twirled around her head as the water and bubbles seeped away.

"And breathe out," continued the book dreamily, giving a blissful sigh.

The wizard pulled Nine towards a narrow, wooden staircase in the back corner of the bookshop.

"Now, Madam," said Flabberghast, "the MORTAL section is down here, in the very bowels of the bookshop."

"Charming."

"Are you ready?"

Nine nodded, wondering what battle she was about to face. But she took a deep breath. And down they went.

CHAPTER 17

Abandoned cobwebs dangled above the stairway, some so large that strands draped down onto Nine's face as she walked. Clearly not many witches and wizards were that interested in mortal books. Nine tried to ignore the wails, smashes and splashes coming from the shop floor behind them as she stepped down the staircase. It was dark, but the steps were lit by candles sitting in little carved alcoves in the wall. Nine was pleased the candles didn't appear to be talking ones – there was enough noise already.

As they went further and further down the staircase, the noises from the shop floor grew more distant and the room grew colder.

"I've never ventured down here before," said Flabberghast in a hushed voice. "These are all books from your world."

"Why would they be here in Beyond – *The Mystery of Wolven Moor*, and other books from my world?" Nine asked.

Flabberghast shrugged. "My people travel the realms, all the worlds and the Worlds Between Worlds. Your world is merely one of them."

Nine walked off the last step. A damp, musty smell hung in the air. She was about to step into the cellar when Flabberghast flung out an arm.

"Be careful, Madam," he whispered. "Your best chance is to sneak up on the book. Catch it unawares."

Nine nodded. A little current of excitement ran through her body and the smallest of smiles appeared on her face. The game was on. And the prize, for some reason, was her favourite book.

Nine stepped forward. A floorboard creaked. She held her breath.

Nothing.

She widened her eyes in the gloom, trying to read the categories labelling each of the sleeping shelves.

HISTORY.

FANTASY.

Her eyes lit up.

MYSTERY.

There it was. She crept towards her favourite shelf: mystery tales. Stories where answers were hidden and secrets unravelled and where, perhaps, for a moment, anything was possible. Her mind travelled back to the library in the land she had once called home, where the gentle, ginger-haired librarian Mr Downes would let her sneak in and "borrow" books that helped her escape the grey misery of her life. In so many ways, she owed him so much. Her heart burned as she remembered again how she had stolen from him.

She trailed her fingertips in the air, an inch away from the soft, dark binding of the books as she passed.

Her heart thumped as her fingers stopped at a brown spine with gold lettering. *The Mystery of Wolven Moor* by Horatio Piddlewick.

Yes! She had nearly succeeded. None of the other books had noticed her thieving feet tiptoe closer in the shadows. None of them had noticed her thieving hand reach for its prize.

She stretched her fingers around the book, eased it out gently, silently and—

"Caught you," whispered Mr Downes' voice in her ear.

For a moment, Nine's heart leapt into her mouth, her fingers fumbled at the book, and it fell towards the floor. Just in time, her hand shot out and caught it.

The books remained unaware.

And she realised, with a pang, that the voice was not real. *Was it?* No. *It couldn't be.* It was just her mind playing tricks on her, surely. Just a shadow of a memory – the memory of the dear librarian with his gingery hair and horn-rimmed spectacles. The librarian who had caught her and saved her. Nine gave a small, sad smile as she wondered what on earth he would make of her now, in a magical bookshop at the Back of Beyond.

"Well done, Madam!" whispered Flabberghast, beckoning her back.

"Wait," said Nine. She looked around desperately. *Ma's item. The safekeeping…*

"Come on, make haste!"

There must be some clue! Something! Anything!

"MADAM!"

Nine backed away from the bookshelf, not taking her eyes off the books in case they suddenly sprang to life. But there was nothing – no clue, no sign. Her heart felt empty. She would never know what important thing her ma had left behind.

They walked backwards slowly all the way to the narrow staircase, then sprinted up as fast and as quietly as they could.

The further and higher they went, the louder the noise and the chaos they could hear from the shop floor. Nine tucked her book inside her satchel, and her fingers brushed against the witch's secret jar. Surely it wouldn't be long before Ophidia arrived, and Nine would somehow have to get everyone into the Secret Shop...

"They're going to get me!" moaned Bonehead, running past them, furiously chased by twenty books replying, "No, we're not! We have every confidence in you!"

"Whoever that shopkeeper is, he needs to get back here and sort this shop out!" said Nine, running over to Eric, who was about to be covered in custard from a jug dangled threateningly above his head. She scanned the shelves, searching desperately through all the cookbooks starting with a letter P... *PERFECT PANCAKES*! There it was!

Nine reached out her hand, but immediately got knocked by Cas, still clinging on to her somewhat deflowered hat, and being chased by a book scattering lavender everywhere.

The custard was just about to pour.

"Eric! Your book!" Nine shouted triumphantly, pulling the pancake-shaped tome from the shelf and thrusting it into Eric's hands.

"Ohhhhh," sulked the other books in disappointment. Then they all flew back onto the shelves, and the custard, raining cherries and ladles of stew all vanished in an instant.

"I have mine too!" declared Bonehead from the other side of the shop. Nine saw him wave a book in the air and then tuck it into his ribcage.

"Knew you could do it," the book replied to him, as the others slunk back sulkily to their shelves muttering about stupid, useless skeletons.

"I am just TEMPORARILY unemployed," growled Cas, stomping by, dragging her book and her now flowerless hat behind her. "And I DON'T need to relax!"

"But where's *your* book, Flabberghast?" said Nine. "We've all got ours."

"First floor," said Flabberghast, pointing to the staircase Bonehead had run up earlier. "Make haste, everyone. Let's go and get it so we are ready before—"

The front door of the shop crashed open.

"Before Ophidia the Unpredictable comes?" said Nine and swallowed hard.

188

There stood Ophidia, narrowing her purple eyes at them. "If I were you, *dear*," she called to Flabberghast, as she dropped her coin into the honesty box, "I would stay out of my way or so help me, I will turn you all into—"

"Ah! Now you," piped up the honesty box, "you really need to learn to control your temper, mate."

"Out of my way!" she roared to the box and sent it flying with a swipe of her hand. The box smacked into a shelf, knocked it wonky, and the complete HOUSE MAINTENANCE section slid down into a pile on the floor.

"I recommend," said the honesty box in a dizzy voice, "*The Calm Guide to Temper Tantrums*—"

"Silence, fool!"

"By Millicent the Permanently Unflustered."

Ophidia growled. "Another word and I will burn this entire bookshop to the ground!" She opened wide her arms under her emerald cloak and floated up into the air. Then she swooped towards the staircase, flying over the heads of Nine, Flabberghast and the others, deliberately knocking off Flabberghast's hat as she did so.

"Temper, temper," whispered the honesty box defiantly, floating itself back into position by the front door.

Nine and Flabberghast looked at each other as Ophidia entered the room on the first floor. The sounds of crashing and shouting began, with occasional bursts of emerald sparks shooting out of the doorway above them.

"Do you think she still has Dish and Spoon in her cloak?" asked Nine.

"I do not doubt it," said Flabberghast, pulling his hat back down on his head. "Surely she would not part with such a prize!"

"Listen," Nine said, lowering her voice. "I've got a plan. While Ophidia is distracted with the books, I'm going to grab Dish and Spoon—"

"You're going to do *what*?" gasped Flabberghast.

"You get your book, get the others out and meet me by the door to the Secret Shop of Secrets."

Flabberghast looked flabbergasted. "You want me to just 'meet you' by a shop door," he said in an unnaturally high-pitched voice, "when you have just robbed my aunt – who is a little on the I-will-burn-this-entire-bookshop-to-the-ground side?" He grabbed handfuls of his curly hair. "Madam, this is preposterous! You will get us all killed. What in the name of strawberry tea can you be thinking?"

Nine looked at him straight. "I – I can't tell you. I'm sorry. But will you trust me?"

Flabberghast looked worried and unsure.

Thief. Liar. Traitor.

Above them came another crash, an angry roar and a small staircase-shaking explosion, followed by green smoke puffing out of the first-floor doorway.

"Will you trust me?" Nine pleaded, grabbing Flabberghast's sleeve. "You said you would trust me with your life!"

Flabberghast stared at her searchingly, then nodded.

Nine nodded back and then sprinted up the staircase, with Flabberghast, Eric, Bonehead and Cas following behind. She had pickpocketed a witch before. It would surely all be fine. Except this was the most unpredictable witch in all the realms. Her heart pounded as they turned towards the doorway. She took a deep breath and stretched her fingers.

She was on in *three...*

Oh, she hoped this didn't get them killed.

Two...

Focus on the prey.

She couldn't see anything but green smoke.

One...

GO!

CHAPTER 18

Nine charged into the room with the others close behind, waving her hands to clear the emerald smoke.

The walls were lined with more piles of books, bookshelves and even book-filled buckets hanging from the ceiling on long ropes. There was a stream of green sparkles as Ophidia blasted a book across the room, where it fell in a heap in the bargain bin.

"You have to count to ten," explained another book patiently, floating beside her. Large, puffy, purple numbers from one to ten began popping up all around Ophidia.

"Out of my way!" Ophidia said, clawing at the numbers furiously with her green-painted fingernails.

Nine saw her opportunity. It was now or never. She tensed her legs and launched at Ophidia's back, reaching for the cloak fastened around her neck. But her fingers slipped, and Ophidia spun around, throwing Nine to the ground.

Ophidia spun around. "How dare you!" she roared, her fingertips glowing green. Sparks shot out at Nine, who dashed behind a bookshelf, which promptly exploded into green smoke, sending books flying in every direction.

"Gahh!" cried Flabberghast. "That was the BEGINNERS MAGIC section!" He began rummaging around furiously amongst the scattered books. "*Wizardry for Complete Beginners Who Are Utterly Terrible and Awful and Rubbish!* Where are you?"

"Buy me!" said another book to Ophidia. "I have loads of suggestions. Like breathe into a paper bag!" A massive pink paper bag fastened itself over Ophidia's face, covering her eyes. Ophidia gave a muffled yell and clawed at the bag with her fingers.

Seizing the opportunity, Nine leapt for Ophidia's back again and this time her fingers grabbed the silky material, and she tore it from Flabberghast's aunt with a sickening ripping sound. Nine tumbled back down to the floor, the cloak in her hands, and dashed behind another bookshelf.

Ophidia let out a roar of rage and tore the pink bag from her face. She turned to find Nine, twisted her wrists, fingertips ready—

"Oh no you don't, Missus!" said Cas. She plonked her hat on her head, charged forward and crashed into Ophidia's knees, sending her plummeting face down to the floor.

"Try getting a massage!" called out a dozen books at the same time. And they leapt onto Ophidia's back, pummelling up and down with their hefty spines.

Ophidia let out a roar of frustration and sent green threads rushing forward, exploding the bookshelf Nine was hiding behind. Nine screamed as she was knocked backwards and saw that more green threads were heading straight for her – quickly wrapping around her leg and dragging her back towards Ophidia. She clung on to the cloak, sliding it along the floor and thrusting it towards Bonehead, who grabbed it in his bony fingers.

"Bonehead! Get the cloak out of the shop!" Nine cried. "Wait outside!"

The skeleton legged it to the door, with his book shouting from his ribcage, "That's the spirit! Go, go, go!"

Eric lumbered into view. "Help Lady!" he cried determinedly. He grabbed Nine's arm and dragged her towards him, as Ophidia's green strands tugged her in the opposite direction.

"Don't you dare!" bellowed Ophidia. She sent a green, sparking shockwave of power along her body which sent the massaging books flying across the room.

"Madam!" called Flabberghast as a book flew up to his face.

"I'll teach you how to use magic without even using your hands!" the book crowed, as rope appeared from nowhere and fastened itself around the wizard's wrists.

"Madam, I am not entirely sure things are going according to plan!"

"Don't worry," said a cheery book next to the wizard. "I'll teach you how to fly like a bird in one easy step."

Suddenly Flabberghast was up in the air, upside down. "Definitely not going according to plan, Madam!"

"We've got the cloak!" yelled Nine. "Find your book and get out!"

"And how, Madam, do you propose I do that with my wrists tied and hanging UPSIDE DOWN?"

Eric tugged on Nine desperately.

"You dare steal my cloak!" roared Ophidia, as the green strands around Nine's leg grew in number and climbed higher and higher up her body, wrapping around her chest, her neck...

Nine's hand flew to her throat. Her breath ... was being ... squeezed ... out...

"Then I shall steal your life!"

"A brilliant way to calm down when your temper is rising..." said a book, which dropped next to Ophidia.

"IS A GROUP HUG!" chorused twenty open books, which all hurtled themselves at Ophidia, burying her in a papery, book-hugging pile.

All the green threads surrounding Nine speedily unravelled and vanished as Ophidia tried desperately to fight off the insistently attacking, hugging books. Nine gasped, coughed and touched her throat, then struggled to her feet. As she stood up, her eyes were level with the little round window. She saw Bonehead standing outside, holding the cloak and waving.

"RUN!" said Nine, grabbing Eric's hand and pulling him towards the door. Eric's other hand grabbed Cas by her mottled, grey arm. "Flabberghast!" Nine yelled.

Suddenly, the wizard came crashing to the ground, landing head first in a huge pile of books. He flustered his way to the surface.

"You really are Utterly Terrible and Awful and Rubbish, aren't you?" sighed a book next to him.

Flabberghast grabbed it awkwardly with his bound hands and let out a cry of joy. "Found it!" He leapt to his feet and the ropes around his wrists slunk off sulkily.

"Come on!" yelled Nine, as green sparks started to zap the hugging books one by one across the room.

Nine's heart thumped as she thought about where they were heading next. They all ran down the staircase, with Ophidia's roars getting louder and more furious. They ran onto the shop floor. There was the front door. They had nearly made it... Past the last stacks of books... Nearly!

The front door opened itself politely. Flabberghast overtook and darted outside.

"Thank you for visiting the bookshop. Please do come again," said a gentle voice with a loud, exasperated sigh.

A voice.

She.

Now.

Knew.

Nine stopped in her tracks, as Eric thudded into her and Cas thudded into him. Nine turned around and stared in disbelief.

A flickering, almost see-through image of a man in a brown cloak and brown pointy hat, with gingery hair, horn-rimmed spectacles...

"Mr Downes?" Nine gasped as the spell faded into nothing.

"Make HASTE, Madam!" cried Flabberghast, as he steered the cloak-carrying Bonehead towards where the invisible Secret Shop of Secrets should be.

"That's Mr Downes!" Nine cried, pointing at where the faint figure had been. "The librarian from my world!"

Eric moved in front of her and dragged her along the cobbled stones.

"It's not your librarian!" Flabberghast shouted, as they approached the doorway to the Secret Shop of Secrets. "It's the old bookseller!"

"Well," said Nine, her brain whirring, "they appear to be the same person!"

Flabberghast stopped and looked thoughtful. "He left suddenly. Mysteriously. No one knows where he went."

"I do!" said Nine.

The two of them stared at each other, until an almighty SMASH of shattering glass from the first-floor bookshop window drew their attention back. A whoosh of furious emerald sparks cascaded out, swirling angrily in the air and landing in front of them. They took the form of Ophidia the Unpredictable.

"My cloak!" she raged.

"Deep breaths," squeaked a book floating behind her.

"Open the door!" screamed Nine.

"Where IS the door?" wailed Flabberghast, his hands frantically reaching for the handle.

Nine ran towards it, desperately searching, but the door opened for them, and Flabberghast, Nine, Eric, Cas and Bonehead ran inside as far as they could, skidding to a halt in the endless gloom. A split second later a whoosh of emerald pieces hurtled after them into the shop—

And the door of the Secret Shop Of Secrets clicked quietly shut behind them.

CHAPTER 19

SHHH appeared in red letters on the doormat behind them as the emerald pieces whooshed past and re-formed into the shape of Flabberghast's furious aunt.

"I will take that, you fools!" Ophidia bellowed. A flick of the wrist, and the green strands whisked the cloak from Bonehead's grip and back into Ophidia's hand. "And for your punishment, there will be consequences..." Her fingertips sparkled green but—

SHHH. The letters had lifted from the doormat and were weaving frantically around Ophidia, who frowned.

"How dare you silence me!" Ophidia said to the shop.

"Oh, come now, that's no way to speak to your niece," came a smooth, lava-like voice.

Ophidia narrowed her eyes and raised an eyebrow. Nine felt Flabberghast stiffen beside her.

"Ohhhhhh dear."

SHHH.

The scarlet letters wove around Flabberghast now.

"Trust me. Please," Nine whispered to the wizard.

"Who's she, then?" said Cas to Bonehead.

"Brother dear," said the witch, stepping out of the shadows before Bonehead could answer. "And Auntie dear. Oh, I adore family reunions. I brought sandwiches." She smirked as a plate of sandwiches appeared out of nowhere and hovered in the air between them.

"His sister?" said Cas, lifting the brim of her hat.

"We're doomed," whispered back Bonehead.

"So this is your thriving business that you spoke of," Ophidia said approvingly. "Clever girl."

"She is NOT clever," hissed Flabberghast, flapping irritably and blowing at the SHHH letters that swarmed around him.

The witch strutted over and stood next to her aunt. "Oh, but I am. Am I not, Auntie dear? And perhaps you could use a clever partner in your quest

201

to make, and wield" – she looked her aunt square in the eye – "*gold*."

Nine watched nervously as Ophidia held her niece's gaze, her senses on high alert for any threatening movement from the two terrifying witches. Flabberghast's aunt might be the most unpredictable witch in all the realms, but his sister was surely the most untrustworthy. And all of Nine's hopes rested on her.

"Perhaps I could," Ophidia replied at last. "I dare say you'd be far more help than those foolish alchemists."

"How dare you!" burst out Flabberghast. "They were the best in the business!"

Everyone looked at Flabberghast with raised eyebrows, except Bonehead, who tried his hardest.

"Well," said Flabberghast awkwardly, "they were … in the business."

Ophidia tutted at him, patted the emerald cloak and swished it back around her shoulders.

"The insolent alchemists know too much, Auntie, do they not? As your new partner, I could dispose of them—"

"No, you blimmin' won't!" Cas cried, lowering her head and preparing to charge at the witch.

Nine reached out and held her back with both arms. "No, wait," she hissed and bit her lip. This was clearly part of the witch's plan – but was it part of Nine's?

Ophidia reached inside her cloak and pulled out the little Dish and Spoon. She presented them on her palm to her niece, who picked them up with her scarlet-painted fingernails and smiled her cold smile. An uncorked secret jar appeared beside her and she tipped Dish and Spoon in.

Nine's heart leapt.

"Wait, what are you doing?" Flabberghast yelled. His fingertips sparkled silver and his broken magic fizzled out. "You are the worst sister in all the realms!" He ran directly at her, but Nine had no arms left to grab him.

The witch rolled her eyes and a scarlet thread shot from one lazy fingertip, hitting Flabberghast in the stomach, and sending him flying backwards on his bottom. "Not now, brother dearest," she said. "I'm busy."

The cork flew into the jar's open top, then the jar whooshed up towards the shelves, so high that it vanished from view.

"Well," sighed the witch, flicking back her scarlet hair and grabbing another sandwich from the plate

203

still floating near by. "Isn't this turning out to be a rather eventful day?"

"At least it can't get any worse," Flabberghast hissed to Nine, as Eric pulled him to his feet.

Suddenly the door to the Secret Shop flung open and a huge spiral of mauve-sparkled wind swept through the room. Nine's satchel flew up and hit her in the face. Ophidia's cloak was swept over her head. Cas's hat flew up in the air, and the secret jars rattled and clinked together.

"Aha!" exclaimed a dramatic voice. "I, Gazillion the Unstoppable, am here!"

"I take that back," muttered Flabberghast.

"Turnip wizard!" said Eric, his eyes wide.

Gazillion pointed his finger at the troll. "I," he announced, "am not a turnip."

"More's the pity," muttered everyone else in the room at the same time.

"I," continued Gazillion, ignoring them, "will prove myself to be the most powerful wizard in all the realms."

"What are you talking about, boy?"

"Too long have I been your underling, Ophidia the Unpredictable!" raged Gazillion, his face becoming more purple as he went on. "Too long have I faced peril in your stead! Braving the Hopscotch Championship to reach the Tower! Braving the Tower to find the whereabouts of Professor Dish!"

Ophidia threw Gazillion an unimpressed look. "You foolish boy! I told you to get me an alchemist who could make Stargold! It's your fault you lost her again! Now, enough of this nonsense. I am the one who possesses the formula, and once it is made, it is I who will be the most powerful in all the realms!"

Her fingertips glowed emerald.

"But there is something you do not know!" said Gazillion, flinging his arms wide dramatically. "I Gazillion, have studied your methods, Ophidia the Unpredictable, and so I—"

He stopped abruptly and pointed his fingers at Ophidia. There was a sudden burst of a dozen mauve strands from Gazillion's hands, which wrapped themselves around Ophidia, catching her by surprise and knocking her to the ground.

"See?" crowed Gazillion, clapping his hands, and dancing on the spot in delight. "See?! I tricked you! I didn't finish my sentence! I attacked you instead! You weren't expecting that, were you? I was unpredictable! Unpredictable!"

Ophidia let out a roar so loud it made the secret jars rattle. The mauve strands that bound her pinged off and vanished. Gazillion stopped dancing.

Flabberghast's sister floated up in the air and seemed to sit down on an invisible chair, her legs crossed. The tray of sandwiches zoomed up beside her.

"Ooh, how marvellous. I do adore a spot of backstabbing in the afternoon." She looked at Nine, then pointedly picked up a sandwich and took a mouthful.

Nine felt her stomach tighten. Had she been taken for a fool? Fallen into the witch's trap? Was she about to be stabbed in the back as well?

A zap of green was aimed at Gazillion but he leapt to the side. It ricocheted off a wall and went shooting upwards into the darkness—

And hit a secret jar with a heart-stopping SMASH.

Everyone froze for a moment, as amber letters tumbled down into the shop, twisting and turning, trying to organise themselves into words, muttering in a voice that sounded like Flabberghast's, "I ate my sister's entire birthday cake and blamed it on her dragon."

Flabberghast swallowed hard and shot a quick look up at his sister, who narrowed her eyes in

206

return. Gazillion seized the moment and sent a mauve thread back at Ophidia. She deflected it with a blinding flash of emerald, then she and Gazillion stood facing each other, their eyes wide and fierce. The calm before the storm…

"Yes, I have a feeling this is going to get messy," said Flabberghast, grabbing Nine and Eric and shoving them further along the wall of the shop.

There was an explosion of flashes of mauve and emerald, lighting up the shop and the shelves — shooting left, right, above, around — causing crashing and smashing as they ricocheted off walls or were deflected by their opponent.

One went flying upwards again, causing a shelf to come hurtling in Nine's direction, and she ducked as it hit the wall behind her with an almighty *thomp*. Nine looked upwards. Dish and Spoon were somewhere up there, out of sight and out of reach. Had she just led her friends into danger? All for nothing?

Gazillion and Ophidia both flew up into the air, twisting and spiralling around each other, shooting strands of magic at each other's limbs.

"Dear, dear. Such a shame when friends fall out," said the witch, ducking slightly as Gazillion went hurtling over her head. She casually placed her half-eaten sandwich back on the tray. "Shall we make it a little more interesting?"

Her smile disappeared, and with a twist of her wrist, scarlet threads shot into Ophidia's cloak and snatched the two halves of the formula before Ophidia could react. The parchments floated in mid-air, suspended above Gazillion and Ophidia. Everyone stared at the parchment, then followed the scarlet threads back to the witch.

"Give me that formula!" they yelled together.

Then in a whirl of colour, emerald and mauve sparks shot around wildly, illuminating the darkened room. They clambered over each other, pulling each other back, shooting colourful threads wildly in an attempt to reach the parchments first.

Nine grabbed Eric and Cas and pulled them further back into a corner of the room.

"I say," said Bonehead, "this is rather exciting. Takes me back to the Hopscotch Championship of 1831." He creaked his head slowly around to look at Flabberghast with non-existent eyes. Flabberghast ducked as an emerald streak of magic shot just above his head.

"It's nothing of the sort," he scoffed.

"Come on – what exactly *did* happen at the Hopscotch Championship of 1831?" said Nine.

"Must we speak of this now?" groaned Flabberghast.

"Do you know, I rather think we should," said Bonehead pointedly.

"Well?" said Nine.

Flabberghast grimaced. "Aldous the Gloom-Stricken—"

"Bonehead, you mean?"

"Aaaaaaand myself," continued Flabberghast, "were on square six, under attack from the formidable Firework Flower. Regretfully" – the wizard glanced at the skeleton – "I have allergies, Madam, including certain pollens. And unfortunately, at the time of greatest peril when our survival was in the balance, when there was a moment of terrible, tense silence as the Firework Flower poised for its final, deadly attack—"

"Did you sneeze?"

Flabberghast squirmed. Nine turned to Bonehead.

"You died because he sneezed?"

"Oh, it was the most terrible, violent, loudest sneeze I have ever heard," said Bonehead woefully. "It scared the life out of me."

"For which," Flabberghast said, taking a breath and looking the skeleton in the eye sockets, "I deeply apologise."

"Oho!" said Bonehead, standing straighter than Nine had ever seen him. He seemed to grow another two inches.

"Bonehead!" said Nine, as emerald sparks hit the wall and bounced furiously around the room.

"Ooh, I've been waiting a long time to hear that." Bonehead wiggled his fingers joyously.

"Bonehead! Get down!"

"It doesn't matter. I'm already dead, thanks to the boy's nose," boomed Bonehead. "What more could happen?"

Mauve sparks hit his skull and sent it flying off his shoulders and across the room.

"Ah," said Bonehead's skull from somewhere in the shadows.

"Oh, for crying out loud!" Nine muttered.

She looked over to see Gazillion being forced to spin around on the spot, the parchments being teased higher and higher at the end of the scarlet strands.

"You double-crossing devil!" Ophidia roared at her niece.

The witch held up a scarlet-fingernailed hand in protest. "Triple. Possibly more. I've stopped counting."

"You will not escape the consequences, girl!"

Gazillion stopped spinning, and blasted Ophidia

with mauve sparks, sending her flying backwards into the wall.

The witch just smiled and picked up another sandwich. "We'll see."

"Witch ... clever?" wibbled Eric, wringing his tail.

"Witch a pain in the backside," said Nine.

"A little help?" boomed Bonehead's skull from across the room.

Nine sighed. "Stay here," she said to the others.

"Madam! Is that wise?" protested Flabberghast, holding tight to his hat as an emerald flash flew overhead.

"Do you think we'll ever hear the end of it if I don't?" Nine snapped, and she dashed across the floor in the vague direction of the skull. She hunched over as emerald and mauve flashed around her, wondering not for the first time what the other thieflings in Pockets' gang would think if they could see her now – fighting *for* her friends, *for* her family, instead of against the whole world. She felt a stab of pity for the thieflings as she realised they would never have what she had.

"Bonehead!" she called.

"Over here!" boomed Bonehead's voice. "Although, I'm not entirely sure where 'here' is."

Fortunately, an ominous green light revealed a skull on its side in the dark, a few arm-lengths away. Nine threw a look over her shoulder. Gazillion and Ophidia were both flying wildly around the room, getting higher and higher, shooting magic at each other with one hand, and trying to grab the dangling parchments with the other.

Nine darted towards the skull, reached out and grabbed it.

"Seriously? Because he sneezed?"

"Never mind that now! Everything's upside down!" moaned Bonehead.

A shot of mauve missed Nine by an inch. Her heart skipped a beat. She needed to get out of here before anything worse happened...

SMASH! Nine froze for an instant, then looked up and saw a secret jar smashed on the floor, and crimson words whispering and murmuring all around.

"Shame," said the witch, as she brushed sandwich crumbs from her dress. "That was a good one."

DEATH read the crimson letters as they reached Nine and swirled around her, murmuring the word again and again. "Oh, pack it in!" She swooshed her free hand at the word and dashed back across to the others.

"Madam!" hissed Flabberghast. "We must leave this place before we *all* have our heads knocked off!"

"For once, I agree with the boy," boomed Bonehead, as Nine plonked the skull back on top of the skeleton's body. It fused together with a sickening click.

Another jar smashed, showering shards of glass everywhere. STOLEN … LOCKET … GOOD MAN floated the words, murmuring in Nine's voice as they whirled around. Nine felt sick. She glanced around to check no one else had realised it was hers. Only the witch was watching and sent Nine a little knowing smile.

"Jars smash!" said Eric. "Save Spoon!" He put his fingers on his bark-like cheeks and his yellow eyes grew wide. "Spoon friend!"

"Yes, Spoon friend," said Nine fiercely. "And we're not leaving without him."

She looked in despair in the direction of the shelves.

Another shower of sparks sent a jar wobbling precariously and hurtling to the ground with a SMASH.

"They could be anywhere up on those shelves!" she said.

"Good job you got someone what can climb well, ain't it?" said Cas. She squared up her little stony shoulders. "Still not what I signed up for, though."

"Better get used to it," said Nine, with a sigh. "This is pretty much a normal day for us."

"So it blimmin' seems." Cas raised a stony eyebrow, took off her hat and handed it to Nine. She took a deep breath, then hurtled across the emerald-and-mauve-lit floor on her little, stocky legs, her elbows rocking from side to side as she dodged the magic. Nine watched as Cas reached the shelves and, with incredible ease for someone so short and well built, climbed her way up the shelves, examining the jars as she went.

More smashes. More secrets whispering and muttering as blue, purple, gold and green letters rushed around, organising themselves into words. Ophidia and Gazillion had now floated back down and were hurling each other repeatedly into the walls.

"You're a new one," Flabberghast's sister said thoughtfully, still sitting in mid-air. She watched as Cas climbed ever higher up the shelves, then she released the scarlet grasp on the formula and let the parchment float down slowly towards the ground. "You must be yet another of my brother's waifs and strays," the witch called to Cas, shrugging. "Well, he has spares." Her fingertips glowed scarlet.

"No!" A surge of panic shot through Nine, catapulting her legs into action. Nine ran in the witch's direction, her satchel thumping against her side.

"Got it!" Cas called down from a high shelf, brandishing a jar.

Nine had nearly reached Flabberghast's sister, but without even turning to look, the witch shot scarlet threads in Nine's direction. The blow hit Nine in the chest and threw her backwards. She flopped onto the floor, gasping for a moment, then scrambled dizzily to her feet.

Why had she been stupid enough to trust the witch?

But it was too late.

CHAPTER 20

The witch pointed at Cas. Scarlet threads hit the shelf, knocking one of the brackets underneath. The shelf tilted down, and all the jars began to slide off – crashing to the ground with ear-splitting smashes. Cas lost her balance and her grip on the jar. The jar hurtled towards the floor – and so did Cas.

"Whoops," said the witch lightly, examining a scarlet fingernail.

"FRIENDS!" came the wail of a heartbroken troll behind Nine.

Eric dashed past her, flinging out his arms, catching a gargoyle with one huge hand and a glass jar containing a dish and a spoon in the other.

Nine stared at him in amazement, although Eric looked more surprised than everyone.

"Eric ... save?" He looked at the jar and the gargoyle. "Eric save! Eric save!" Then he caught the witch's eye, straightened up and held his head proudly. "Troll clever."

The witch rolled her eyes melodramatically as more secret jars rained down and smashed around her. Letters of every colour hurled around the room, like a swarm of bright, angry insects, diving at their heads and whispering furiously.

"Get off! Get away!" cried Nine, using the gargoyle's hat to swipe at a crowd of indigo letters that were dive-bombing her, muttering how they had accidentally eaten their uncle's favourite cloak.

Gazillion yelled as a lime-green secret attacked him as he attempted to send a wave of mauve threads towards Ophidia, who was herself being bombarded by bright pink letters confessing they'd melted their grandmother's cauldron while attempting to make a particularly spicy soup.

As the ever-increasing chaos swept around the shop, Nine looked up into the air and saw the witch raise an eyebrow and rise up from her invisible seat. An empty, bulbous, uncorked jar appeared beside her. Hastily she whispered something into the jar, which filled with jiggling, pushing scarlet letters, then she sent it whooshing upwards and out of sight towards the shelves cloaked in darkness.

A moment later, a tall, narrow secret jar drifted down from the shadows, again with scarlet letters swirling around – *a secret exchanged for a secret.* That was the magical rule. Nine narrowed her eyes. What was the witch up to? Which secret was in the tall, narrow secret jar that the witch had urgently wanted ... or perhaps wanted to protect?

As the threads of magic disappeared back into the witch's fingertips, the tall secret jar began to shrink, until it was no bigger than a finger. The witch clutched it in her hand and tucked it up inside the long sleeve of her crinoline dress.

"STARGOLD WILL BE MINE!" Gazillion roared. His mauve-sparkling fingertips stretched towards the pieces of formula parchment, which were being buffeted through the air, pushed and shoved by all the secrets.

"Go!" Flabberghast called to Eric. "Take Cas and the jar and go! I shall deal with my wretched family!"

"No! Lemme at that blimmin' witch!" said Cas, wriggling in Eric's grasp. The troll struggled to hold both the gargoyle and the jar. "Cas, stop!" he said firmly.

"Allow me," said Bonehead. He patted his ribcage, which contained the book, then took the jar from Eric and Cas's hat from Nine. "It's rather nice to be helpful."

The troll lolloped towards the front door, both arms gripping Cas, who was kicking her little stony legs in mid-air as they left the Secret Shop, shutting the door behind them.

"MINE!" Ophidia yelled over a swarm of noisy, muttering multi-coloured letters. She stretched out her fingers for the parchment too.

"Madam, we must leave!" Flabberghast said urgently, pulling her arm.

But in that moment, Gazillion and Ophidia sent out a furious wave of mauve and emerald magic at precisely the same time. The magic met in the middle, pushing back and forth against each other. It seemed to steal all the air from the room.

Flabberghast and Nine stared open-mouthed. Miraculously surviving secret jars clinked together from the high shadows, louder and louder, as if they were shaking violently on their miraculously surviving shelves.

Ophidia and Gazillion wore faces of rage as the waves of emerald began to push down the mauve. Gazillion's rageful expression twisted into panic.

"What is she going to do to him?" gasped Nine.

"I suggest we don't find out," said Flabberghast, dragging her towards the door through hundreds of multi-coloured letters.

Nine looked behind her to see Gazillion's eyes full of fear and Ophidia's full of furious delight as they both realised Gazillion would lose.

"Foolish boy!" whooped Ophidia. "You dare to challenge me! But no one will ever be as unpredictable as—" A band of scarlet suddenly whooshed across the shop. There was a blinding explosion of white as the three strands met. Nine looked away, shielding her eyes.

Silence. Even the secrets were quiet.

The white glare faded, and there Nine saw a large turnip in place of Gazillion, and a thousand tiny, slightly confused-looking emerald pieces which grouped together and hovered uncertainly where Ophidia had stood. The two halves of parchment drifted down and landed on the ground.

"A spell that has turned them back to their last physical form!" gasped Flabberghast. "Gazillion was last a turnip..."

"And your aunt turned into emerald pieces to follow us through the door!" said Nine, staring in disbelief.

They looked up at where the scarlet band had come from.

"Bravo. You two really are remarkably quick-witted," said the witch, dusting the crumbs from the final sandwich off her fingers.

Flabberghast quickly removed his hat and leapt up at the still-confused emerald pieces, swooping them into his hat and scrunching the brim of his hat together. As soon as he had done this, the trapped emerald pieces seemed to be thrown into a furious panic. Flabberghast's hat began bulging in different directions – fast and forcefully.

"GAH!" wailed Flabberghast, as he was knocked off his feet onto the floor.

The frantic activity seemed to kick all the colourful secret letters back into action, and they began muttering and swooping furiously around them again.

"Somebody *do* something!" Flabberghast cried, clinging desperately to his hat, as he bounced along the floor on his stomach.

"A jar!" Nine said. "We need a secret jar!"

She looked at the witch. The witch returned her gaze and floated down from the air towards her and Flabberghast.

Nine tensed. Was this it? With Ophidia seemingly defeated, was she about to be betrayed by the witch? She stared defiantly into the deep blue, ancient eyes as the witch landed in front of her.

Nine held her breath.

The witch smiled coldly.

And an empty glass jar and a cork appeared next to Flabberghast, who was still wrestling with his hat. Nine grabbed the jar and held it up to the wizard's hat, and, with an enormous struggle, Flabberghast tipped the furiously whizzing emerald pieces into the jar. Nine grabbed the cork and slammed it in.

"Well done, Madam!" gasped Flabberghast, putting his hat back on his head and getting to his feet.

Nine picked up the jar, watching as the emerald pieces hurled themselves furiously at the glass. A tiny crack appeared. Nine gasped and held the jar at arm's length.

The witch snatched it out of her hand and sent it flying off into the dark depths, in the direction of any shelves that were lucky enough to remain intact.

"If I were you, brother, I'd get your ridiculous House moving before she smashes her way out of that jar," said the witch. "I don't believe it will take her too long. Do you?" She stepped over the turnip and strutted for the front door, her footsteps crunching over the broken glass. Her heeled shoes trod pointedly over the two halves of parchment as she went. Then without looking, she lazily waved her hands behind her, and shot out scarlet sparks to each half of parchment. They disintegrated instantly into charred, scarlet-tinged flakes.

"Whoops," she said lightly, as she waltzed through the doorway, leaving the door wide open, followed by thousands of colourful, excitedly chattering secrets. They whirled and swirled past her as they escaped into the wild.

"That's going to cause a lot of trouble," said Nine.

"Yes, Madam," sighed Flabberghast. "I think you'll find that's what my sister does best."

CHAPTER 21

Nine followed Flabberghast out of the shop, glancing at all the colourful secrets organising themselves into sentences and floating away on the breeze, their distant murmuring and whispering fading into nothing.

The witch was standing by Eric, Bonehead and Cas at the end of the cobbled path near the bookshop. The glass jar containing Dish and Spoon rested on the ground.

"You know," Flabberghast said in a low voice, "it is rather odd my sister showed no interest in the Stargold formula. I rather thought that would appeal. I'm not entirely sure what she's playing at."

I have my sights on something else. Something far

more interesting. Something, as it happens, little thief,
only you can help me with…

Nine said nothing, the thoughts and doubts tumbling around in her head.

"The sooner we leave her behind, the better," Flabberghast whispered, as they approached the others.

"You! You tried to kill me!" Cas said, stony arms on stony hips and a stony finger pointing at the witch. She took her hat back from Bonehead and plonked it on her head crossly.

"Such harsh words!" exclaimed the witch indignantly. "I was merely making life more interesting for you – and me."

Cas sniffed. "Mighta been more interestin' than sittin' on a wall," she said gruffly. "Mighta enjoyed it … a bit."

Nine knelt down beside the jar, hastily uncorked it and gently tipped out Dish and Spoon. "I can't believe you trapped them in a jar!"

The witch flicked back her scarlet hair, coolly. "You asked me to stop my aunt. And so I did."

Flabberghast looked from Nine to the witch. "Wait… *You* asked—? When did you—?"

The witch gave her brother a withering glare. "Do not fret, brother, this is purely a business arrangement."

"Arrangement?! Business?!" He swallowed hard. "Madam," he said in a trying-very-hard-not-to-panic tone, "what have you done NOW?"

"Saved our friends," said Nine. Guilt burned in her heart. "This was the only way. I'm … sorry," she said, and she meant it. "She made me promise not to tell you."

"And asked for what in return?" Flabberghast said, shooting his sister a suspicious glare.

"Our little secret," sang the witch.

Flabberghast sighed heavily and rubbed his hands over his face, then turned to look at the jar with Dish and Spoon, and Nine noticed the frustration and helplessness in his eyes.

"Go on," teased the witch, following his gaze. "Ask me, brother. You know you have to."

Flabberghast clenched his jaw. Their ancient eyes met. One pair frustrated. One pair delighted.

"Fine," said Flabberghast after a moment. "Can you change them back?"

"What's the magic word?" said the witch, smiling sweetly.

"PLEASE," growled Flabberghast.

The witch smirked. "Oh, brother dearest, you really do need to get your magic back, don't you?

This neediness is pathetic. Even *you* would have been able to manage a simple reversing spell, surely?"

She stretched her hands further apart, as if she was pulling on two ends of a long piece of string. Then she twisted her wrists suddenly and thrust her hands out towards Dish and Spoon. Threads of magic shot out, hitting them both and sending a shockwave of scarlet flowing through them.

Nine shouted in alarm, but then watched in amazement as faces slowly began to appear on Spoon and Dish. Spindly arms and legs popped out from Spoon's handle and Dish's bowl.

The witch fixed Nine with a cold smile. "It's as if you don't trust me."

"I don't," said Nine, staring back.

"Very wise, dearest thief. Very wise."

Spoon sat up and rubbed his head. "What the devil happened?"

"Eric save," said Eric proudly. "Not Flabby. Not Lady." He pointed to his chest. "Eric."

Spoon blinked, as if he was only just remembering the events. "Your aunt, lad! Where is she? He reached for the sword in the sheath around his kilt. "I'll give her a lesson!" Spoon turned and caught sight of the witch. He waved his sword around. "And what the devil is SHE doing here? I'll take you all on! I'll—"

But Spoon's shouts were immediately muffled by Dish, who threw her arms around him and squeezed him tightly.

"For so long I sought recognition for my alchemy achievements. But those years we were apart, searching for answers, were the longest of my life. Perhaps there is more to life than magic or being a famous alchemist." She gazed at Spoon. He smiled and his little wooden cheeks turned a definite shade of red.

Flabberghast twisted his mouth doubtfully. "Well, judging by the number of laboratory disasters you two seem to have, I'm not sure you would have been a famous alchemist for entirely the right reasons."

The witch stifled a snort of laughter.

"Anyway," said Flabberghast, clasping his hands together. "I rather think we've earned some strawberry tea. Shall we?" He gestured towards the House Park.

Spoon cleared his throat. "Actually, lad, I won't be joining you."

"What?" said Nine.

"Aye," said Spoon. "I think the time has come for a new adventure." His tiny hand clasped Dish's tiny hand. She smiled.

Flabberghast's face fell for a moment. "Oh?" Then he looked from Spoon to Dish and from Dish to Spoon. "Oh! Oh, I understand, Dr Spoon." He gave a little sigh. "I presume you wish to gather your equipment from the House?"

Spoon shook his head. "I think we've both conducted enough experiments to last a lifetime. I don't need the equipment any more. Dish is all that I need."

Spoon went over to the troll. Eric wiped a tear from his eye with his tail, and then patted Spoon's head. "Spoon friend."

"Aye, and troll is friend, too," Spoon said, hugging his leg. "A good friend."

Spoon went over to Flabberghast and hopped up onto his forearm. "I said I wished I'd never set foot inside the House at the Edge of Magic." He cleared his throat. "But I did nae mean a word of it."

"I am most delighted you joined us, Dr Spoon," said Flabberghast, his eyes sparkling silver once more.

Spoon jumped up onto Nine's shoulder and hugged her neck.

"I'll miss you, Spoon," said Nine, a little surprised at how easily the words came. Her heart felt heavy.

"Keep the lad out of trouble, will you, lass? Don't let him get near any green-horned minotaurs."

"I'll do my best," said Nine.

"We'll be buying one of those message urns before we go," said Spoon. "You know … just in case I need to get in touch … about any of my equipment."

Flabberghast nodded. Then Spoon gave a brief nod to Cas and Bonehead and looked again at Nine. "When you knocked on the door of the House, lass," he said, "you changed everything. Everything."

Nine just nodded. Her throat was tight, and she seemed to have forgotten how to speak.

Spoon gave one last nod to everyone, then he and Dish held hands and skipped away together, through the streets of Beyond.

"They always leave in the end," murmured Flabberghast.

Nine gave another swallow and blinked a few times when she thought no one was looking.

The witch rolled her eyes. "Someone find a handkerchief. This is breaking my heart," she said coldly, but Nine noticed a faint, silvery sparkle in her eyes which quickly faded away.

Flabberghast looked nervously at the witch. "What will happen to the Secret Shop of Secrets?"

"I suppose it will have to close for a while." She looked at the sky, where the last secrets still swirled their way around, looking for ears to whisper into. "I have a feeling there may be a number of dissatisfied customers." She smiled. "I do hope so."

"Then … you'll be on your way?"

"I do have some urgent business that is just desperate for my attention." Then she turned to Flabberghast. "So I'll say goodbye, brother. Until we meet again."

"Which will hopefully be some while," Flabberghast muttered.

The witch turned and walked away, glancing over her shoulder at Nine and casting the smallest wink.

Nine tried to push the witch from her mind and turned to look at the bookshop, in case there was any chance she could return to look for whatever her ma had left. But the sign by the door was quite clear: "CLOSED FOR AGES. NEED TO TIDY UP."

"Well, you lot are a bit like hard work, ain't ya? Knew it was goin' to be a bit more excitin' than sittin' on a wall, but blimey!" said Cas.

Flabberghast sighed. "I think we definitely need a cup of strawberry tea now."

Flabberghast looked at everyone. "Home we go," he said.

"Home," said Nine.

CHAPTER 22

In tired silence, they made their way through the House Park towards the House at the Edge of Magic. Flabberghast opened the front door and they all slumped inside and stood in the hallway.

"I suppose it hasn't been all bad," said Bonehead, pulling his *Positive Thinking for Brainless Skeletons* book from out of his ribcage and flicking through. "I have my fluffy socks, my cushions … and this." He lifted the black cloth on the cage in the hallway and revealed a little dragon skeleton inside. "I think it shall rather" – he picked up the book again, peered closer and pointed with his bony finger to a paragraph – *"raise the spirits looking after a pet"*.

But Nine's spirits weren't raised. She folded her arms. "And the chain and padlock on the cage when it was in the shop, Bonehead? That didn't give you any warning signs?"

"Undoubtedly an overreaction," said Bonehead, waving a bony hand dismissively. "Think on the bright side." He waved his book at her as the dragon skeleton hiccupped, and a tiny green flame darted from its skull.

Nine narrowed her eyes suspiciously.

"We have our shopping," said Flabberghast. "Let us leave this accursed place."

Nine's eyes pinged wide again as something occurred to her. "We can't leave yet," she said. "We owe Alfwin the Indubitably Dubitable the gold and we don't have it. What are the chances we'll get away with it?"

"Ooh," boomed Bonehead hopefully, "you never know. It might be—"

"Impossible," said Flabberghast. "A business like his has spies everywhere. What will we do? We simply do not have the gold, Madam!"

Then a thought struck Nine. "But we do have..."

She ran down the hallway to the kitchen, as her brain danced with an idea. She grabbed the bucket full of orange gloop and marched back past

Flabberghast, who stood with both the door and his mouth open.

"Take gloop?" said Eric, scratching his head with his long fingernail. "Lady clever?"

"Oh, yes," Nine called over her shoulder as she headed for the This-And-That Shop. "Lady clever."

A few minutes later, she plonked down the bucket of orange gloop on Alfwin the Indubitably Dubitable's table, making him jump.

"It's not gold, but it makes stuff look golden," Nine said. "Watch." She reached into the bucket, grimacing as she grabbed a handful of the orange slime. She flicked some at the tail of the cat statue with more than a little satisfaction. It started to shimmer immediately.

"Not gold, but makes it appear so? That's a filthy rotten trick." He gave a half-smirk and a nod. "I think that appeals to me even more."

"Now why doesn't that surprise me? And you'll be pleased to know we have an endless supply." Nine twisted her mouth thoughtfully. "Though I'm not entirely sure anyone knows why."

She gave one last glare at the cat statue. Its eyes shifted to look over Nine's shoulder. She froze for a moment, then whirled around. No one was there.

Nine narrowed her eyes suspiciously at the cat, then the purple lizard croaked one last time as she walked out of the shop.

As she weaved back through the crowded, cobbled streets to the House Park, Nine felt that same feeling of unease, like someone was breathing down her neck. She reached inside her satchel and rested her hand on the music box, just to remind herself it was safe. Still, she was no closer to discovering what her ma had left in safekeeping. She felt a pang at the missed opportunity. She would have given anything – *any*thing – to know more about her ma.

As Nine arrived back at the House, Flabberghast opened the door to her.

"Ah, Madam." He gave a little nod. "Just in time for tea," he said, stepping back to let her into the hallway.

"Tea," said a lava-like voice coming from beside the front door. "My favourite."

Nine spun around to see the witch standing in the doorway.

"Ah brother, we *do* meet again," she said, strutting into the hallway. "How terribly thrilling."

"What?" cried Flabberghast. "What are you doing here?"

"Oh, causing a little trouble," said the witch, examining a scarlet fingernail. "I rather feel like a holiday. I love holidays."

"Holiday? Where?" said Flabberghast sharply. His eyes narrowed. "How?"

"I need to visit the mortal world," said the witch brightly. "Someone owes me a favour."

"No-no-no-no-no," said Flabberghast. "No. You are absolutely *not* coming in here."

The witch smiled sweetly and then looked at Nine. "Are you going to tell him, or shall I?"

Nine grimaced a little. "It was part of the deal in exchange for saving Dish and Spoon from Ophidia. She needs my assistance."

"Assistance!" Flabberghast groaned. "Madam, have you not yet learned that associating with my sister cannot possibly end well? What in the name of the Sometimes Dead were you thinking?"

"I was thinking of our friends," said Nine.

Flabberghast looked at Nine, looked at his sister and sighed heavily. "I would not trust her with so much as a cabbage."

The witch smiled, tilted her head and made a small, mock curtsey.

"Then, please," said Nine, "just trust *me*."

Flabberghast looked at Nine. "You ask a great deal, Madam, but … agreed."

"Such wonderful news, brother," said the witch, shutting the front door behind her. "Speaking of which, I know how your powers can be restored."

"What?!" gasped Flabberghast. "How?"

"All in good time," said the witch airily. "I think we all need a cup of strawberry tea." She stood beside the coat of arms on the wall in the hallway. "Shall I do the honours?"

Without waiting for an answer, she pulled the tongue of the toad on the coat of arms and—

ZA-BAM! Nine felt the strange but now-familiar feeling of her brain being sucked out of the top of her skull. Everything hurtled in a direction she didn't understand but was almost certainly "up". The witch smiled and strutted down the hallway to the kitchen.

"Witch home," said Eric, looking at Flabberghast with wide eyes.

"Yes," said Flabberghast tightly. "Apparently she is."

"Witch trouble!"

"Yes, she definitely is."

"Make tea," said Eric, patting Flabberghast's arm. Then he lolloped towards the kitchen with some urgency, followed by Bonehead and Cas.

"It won't be for long," said Nine. "I just need to help her with something. I'm just … not entirely sure what that is."

"And that, Madam," said Flabberghast, "is precisely what troubles me."

Nine couldn't argue with that. Flabberghast sighed, then headed down the hallway towards the kitchen. "Eric, we need to fix the teapot. Although I have the most horrible feeling that the glue is somewhere in the cupboard under the stairs."

Nine's heart sank as she thought about all the shopping that had just been dumped in there. They all desperately needed a cup of strawberry tea.

Ma's teapot!

"I know where a teapot is," Nine called to Flabberghast, then headed for the plum-carpeted stairs. With every step she took, she became more certain: she would show him the torn parchment pieces and tell him everything about the Safekeeper. If Nine had trusted him and told him earlier, perhaps there would have been a way to find what her ma had left, instead of trying to manage it by herself. Maybe Nine could even persuade him to come back to Beyond and help her look…

Beyond…

So much had happened. So much to think about. Spoon was gone. Mr Downes had owned the bookshop. He was a wizard! All this time, and she had never known. Maybe that's why he had all those books on magic on the highest shelf in the library.

Nine made her way to her ma's bedroom and flopped on the floor beside the bed. She pulled the gold-starred teapot out from under the bed, lifted the lid and heavy-heartedly pulled out all the pieces of parchment. She put the fragments together and watched as the words appeared...

And caught her breath.

Because now they said:

Retrieved with thanks, The SAFEKEEPER

Retrieved? Retrieved?!

Nine's heart leapt. But she hadn't retrieved anything! The only thing she had removed from the bookshop was... Nine thrust her hand inside her satchel and pulled out *The Mystery of Wolven Moor*. She turned the book over, flicked through the pages and gave the book a little shake. Nothing. It was just a book. Unless... What if...?

Nine placed the closed book on the floor and pulled out the music box from her satchel. She held it in front of the book and, with desperate hope in her heart, she began to play the music – backwards.

As she reached the end of the tune, suddenly the book flipped open all by itself, to the map at the front: the wild Wolven Moor. Nine gasped and leaned back further against the bedframe. Something strange was happening. The image of the map on the two pages began to wobble and reshape itself. A new map was appearing in its place.

The moorland mutated and turned into an island, surrounded by a dark sea. With a little *pop*, a lighthouse appeared perched on the clifftop.

Nine's heart raced. This was definitely not the same as the normal book. She reached on the bed behind her and grabbed her mother's copy with "Eliza" written inside the cover. She checked the map. Her mother's copy showed Wolven Moor. With a shaking hand, she played the music box backwards again. Nothing happened. It was just an ordinary book. She grabbed the bookshop copy. There was the lighthouse and the secret map.

This! This was what her ma had hidden away with the Safekeeper? She had done it!

A little shiver went down her spine as she remembered the Safekeeper's words: "*It's not yours... You don't even know what the item is.*" But curiosity was both Nine's weakness and her strength. If her ma had hidden away a map, she wanted to know what it was leading to.

Nine heard footsteps coming towards the bedroom. Hastily, she moved away one piece of the parchment and the words "*retrieved with thanks*" instantly vanished. She shut both copies of *The Mystery of Wolven Moor* and shoved them underneath the bed just as someone opened her door. In strutted the witch. She paused for just a moment when she saw Nine sitting on the floor.

"What are you doing here?" said Nine, her heart thumping. She still didn't trust this witch as far as she could throw her. And beneath that bed, and on that parchment, were two things she very much didn't want an untrustworthy witch to see.

"Oh, don't mind me," said the witch coolly. "There's only one open window in this House when it flies." The witch walked over to the window. "The window that can never be closed." She brushed her fingertips over it thoughtfully and gazed outside at the silvery strands that danced in the blackness. "And the World Between Worlds is the perfect place.

Because it's not like Beyond. Out there, nobody stops. Nobody hears. Nobody finds."

"Nobody finds what?" asked Nine. Something was odd. She stared at the witch with the eyes of a keen pickpocket, watching every move.

The witch took out the tiny secret jar from her sleeve, uncorked it and tipped the scarlet words out of the window as the House zoomed on.

Nine leapt up, desperately trying to make sense of any words as they flew:

SECRETS

POWER

BETRAYED

FRIENDS

LOCKET

CONSEQUENCES

Nine swallowed hard.

She turned to face the witch, but she was looking at the secret jar that Nine had bought at the shop, and which was still standing on the little bedside table. The turquoise letters still swirled around inside.

"You should probably listen to that secret before we land in your world, dearest thief."

"Before we land *where* in my world?" asked Nine.

But the witch just smirked, turned her back and walked over to the door.

Suddenly Flabberghast's exasperated voice floated up the stairs, followed by the endless chatter of a little cheeky voice. "Madam! A TALKING CANDLE?!" he groaned.

"A talking candle?" said the witch, turning round, her eyes gleaming in delight. "Oh, you didn't! Do you not know what a talking candle is?"

"No! What is so bad about a talking candle?!"

"A talking candle is not truly a candle. It's a most mischievous fire sprite that can assume the form of a flame."

Nine froze. "Oh."

"And *you* brought one into the House at the Edge of Magic," continued the witch. "How very strange my brother did not expressly and repeatedly forbid it." She gave a little snort of laughter.

"MADAM!" wailed Flabberghast from downstairs. "IT – HASN'T – PAUSED – FOR – BREATH!"

"Oh," said the witch, with a deep sigh of contentment, "it's marvellous to be home." And she swept out of the room, closing the door behind her.

Grateful for Flabberghast's protests being shut out, Nine turned to look again at the window.

There was no sign of any scarlet letters, no sound of any whispered words. The secret was lost for ever, never to be seen or heard again. Just as the witch had intended.

Nine went over to the little bedside table and the secret jar with its tumbling letters. When she had chosen the jar, it had somehow felt like just the right one.

Nine hastily uncorked the lid of the jar, and the secret whooshed out in a stream of turquoise letters, which dashed around forming their words. A voice began to murmur.

And it was a voice she knew.

"Ma?" whispered Nine.

"I had a special locket. Not an ordinary locket. I don't know why it was for sale in the TAT shop but it was powerful and dangerous, an old family heirloom that once belonged to Ophidia the Unpredictable. It was traded for, then entrusted to me...

...But then I argued fiercely with the one who gave it to me. I arranged for a spell to be put upon it so she could never touch it or use it again. I gave it to the dear bookshop owner, who said he would take it far away and keep it safe. I betrayed the trust of the one who gave it to me. Now ... things can never be the same."

Nine stared at the letters, eyes wide, as a million thoughts began to link in her mind.

The locket…

That had belonged to Ophidia the Unpredictable…

That was powerful and dangerous…

Like Stargold…

Like Dish and Spoon had tried to make for Ophidia to replace the original one that had been lost…

When Uncle Mortimer the Unwise sold it to the This-And-That Shop to pay for Dragon Droppings…

Where someone must have given it to Nine's mother…

Who had betrayed that person's trust and given it to the bookshop owner…

MR DOWNES…

Who worked in the library, and who Nine had pickpocketed all that time ago…

And had taken her prize, the locket that would not open – this precious, dangerous, sought-after locket –

To Pockets' Nest.

Nine slumped down in shock, only vaguely aware of the metal bedframe digging into her back.

The deal with the witch suddenly made sense. *"I have my sights on something else. Something far more interesting. Something, as it happens, little thief, only you can help me with."*

The locket the witch wanted – which Nine had confessed about in her secret – was waiting in the same place it had been all this time, dangling, broken, from a beam in Pockets' Nest.

Nine leaned her head against the bed. They had saved Dish and Spoon. They had escaped Ophidia. But now, Nine feared, not only was Flabberghast's furious aunt going to come after them once she had escaped, which surely she would, but Nine had also accidentally promised the most tricky, clever witch she knew assistance in acquiring something so dangerous that her ma had gone to all the lengths of the realms to hide it years ago. And Nine would bet her strawberry tea that it had something to do with this map.

Nine ran her fingers through her spiky hair. What had she done? The Safekeeper's words came back to haunt her: *"If something's left with the Safekeeper, there's usually more than one person wants it."*

And that very person was travelling with them.

She thought of the wizard, the troll, the skeleton and the gargoyle downstairs – the only family she had – waiting for the teapot so they could make the Finest Tea in All the Realms. And her heart warmed, and her spirits lifted. Because whatever mistake she had made, whatever danger she was in, she knew she could – she would – trust them with any problem, any secret.

She knew with all her heart, perhaps for the first time, she would never, ever be alone again.

And perhaps, at this moment, that was enough.

EPILOGUE

The secret flew out of the window that would never close, word after word. Never to be seen or heard again. No one could ever know.

Everyone has secrets, do they not?

Sometimes deep, sometimes dark,

sometimes well-meaning or long forgotten – buried in hidden places.

But secrets will sleep and bide their time.

Because one day, sooner or later, they will wake – and there will be consequences.

The secrets will come out to play.

And those who patiently wait in the shadows, who watch from the windows, they gather the secrets.

And soon … the game begins.

But what of the deep, dark secret I must tell, that has never been spoken to another soul?

My secret is this:

I was betrayed by my dearest of friends and fiercest of enemies. She cast away a locket of immense value, a family heirloom. And oh, there were consequences.

She left her daughter on the doorstep. I did not open the door. I left the child to the thieves.

So, now I wait in the shadows. I watch from the windows.

And then, when the time is right, I will do what I should have done that day…

I will bring her daughter home, to where she belongs. To where she was always meant to be.

To the House at the Edge of Magic.

One Year Earlier

The young lady dressed in scarlet, with matching scarlet hair, clutched her little beaded bag and gave it a pat. Inside was a treasure. A marvellous, secret treasure. And it was all part of a marvellous, secret plan. A slow smile spread across her face as she walked across the market. She moved over to a fishmonger's stall and cast her keen eyes about.

There she was. The scruffy orphan with the spiky hair, coming out of the library. But something was different. The girl looked downhearted. She had visited the library a few times now, and usually when she came out, her eyes were full of magic and dreams. Not this time. The girl's hand fiddled with something inside her pocket. She looked … guilty.

Strange.

The scarlet lady followed the pickpocket, a few steps behind, hiding in the shadows. Just like a cat: sighting her prey, stalking it quietly, pouncing at the right moment.

Except … she was not ready to carry out her plan. So, she didn't pounce. She let the scruffy girl walk on. Knowing that when the time was right – and it so nearly was – she would make certain their paths would meet, make sure the thief stole the cursed little house from her very own bag. But the time was not yet right. So the scarlet lady cast one more look as the downhearted child turned down Whinney's Passage and headed for the tumbledown terrace. Clutching her beaded bag just a little bit closer, the scarlet lady went on her way. But she did not know that by the time she reached the end of the street, a locket would be strung up in a nearby cellar – an old, broken locket – a prize for an old, broken gang-master, who was too busy ranting about life not bringing you strawberries to notice the engraving on the back.

TO ELIZA
LOVE
BEWILDA

Acknowledgements

Everyone brings their own kind of magic, and when all the different elements blend and spark and fizz together, the spell is complete. It's the same with creating a book. So my thanks go to everyone who has added their own sparkly ingredient into the mix, especially:

Julia Churchill, the Finest Agent in All the Realms, for simply being the Finest Agent in All the Realms.

My editor, Gráinne Clear, for yet again making it so fun to create this book together. Jenny Bish for brilliant copy-editing and for pointing out that "huff" is a great word until it's been used 568 times.

Chloé Tartinville for the wonderful cover design, Rebecca J Hall for typesetting and Rebecca Oram for spreading the word!

Ben Mantle for his absolutely magical illustrations. The imagination and the details are amazing!

I must say thank you to Camilla's Bookshop in Grove Road, Eastbourne – an incredible second-hand bookshop that I visited regularly as a child. It was like entering a treasure trove, especially when I made the adventurous trek down into the basement. That wonderful, chaotic bookshop is the inspiration for the one in Beyond.

Thanks always to Mum for being the most incredible sounding board and loving this world, and to Dad for his encouragement and taking me to Camilla's Bookshop when I was young. Thank you for all the adventures.

And speaking of inspiration, I must also give a special mention to Julia Churchill's cat, Keema. As I was working hard on a chapter of *Bookshop*, I completely accidentally and magically found myself on Twitter and saw a photo of Keema giving the stariest stare in the history of cats. I said to myself that somehow, I would get that into a scene in *Bookshop*. So there it is! A cameo for Keema and a fun lesson for me to not say rash things on Twitter in the middle of writing a novel...

Huge, sparkly thanks to my husband, Alyn, and our motley collection of children for the love, encouragement and endless cups of tea.

And finally, to YOU, the reader – thank you for reading this book and these acknowledgements! May you find magic in the most unexpected of places.

About the Author

Amy Sparkes has been writing since she was five years old but only started taking it seriously after moving to south-west England and starting a family. Her books have appeared on CBeebies storytime and been shortlisted for several book awards, including the Roald Dahl Funny Prize and the BookTrust Best Books Awards for *Do Not Enter the Monster Zoo*. Amy is known as the Story Godmother and runs writing workshops for children's authors, produces the "Writing for Children" pages for the bestselling *Writing Magazine*, and co-founded the *Writing Magazine Children's Book Prize* for developing writers. When she's not writing, Amy enjoys adventures, discovering secret things which might possibly be magical, and drinking lots of tea.

Have you read the whole series so far?

More coming soon…

We'd love to hear what you thought of
The Bookshop at the Back of Beyond!

🐦 #BookshopBeyond
@WalkerBooksUK
@AmySparkes

📷 @WalkerBooksUK